100%
SUCCESS

Basics

*A quick and simple guide
to guaranteed success in
Network Marketing*

Dedicated to
everyone who struggles
with confidence.

Published With Permission

Sound Concepts

782 S Auto Mall Dr. Suite A

American Fork, UT 84003

To order additional copies of this book or other products by Ed Ludbrook in
North America please visit: www.100PercentTools.com or call 888.285.6320

First Published by 100% Success Institute, London, UK www.100percentinstitute.com

Cartoons by Mick Davis

Designed by Lee Kretschmar

ISBN 978-0-9582832-5-0

What would you do if you knew you could not fail….?

Consider this for a moment.

If you were absolutely convinced of success, what actions would you take? How hard would you work in your Network Marketing business?

Ultimate Sponsoring Question:

All over the world the same two questions produce the same basic answers…

'How many people do you think you can sponsor [recruit] into your network?'

The answer is always a very low number such as *'two'* or *'three.'* When you consider the huge number of people looking to make money and the power of a Networking opportunity, this is a ridiculously low figure. The next question is:

'How many people do you think you could sponsor into your network if you <u>knew</u> they would not fail?'

The answer begins with a wide smile and is finished with *'everyone!' 'hundreds!'* or *'millions!'*
What has changed in just ten seconds? It's the same question.
All I added was *'if you knew they would not fail.'*
The difference is that most people do not want to sponsor someone if they believe the person will fail. The **fear of failure** dominates any dream of success.

This is why in Network Marketing **CONFIDENCE in your success** is the key to success.

The 100% Success Strategy will give you that confidence.
100% Success will guarantee you can succeed in this business.

THE 100% SUCCESS STRATEGY

The strategy you use to build a Network Marketing business is like the foundations of a house, it provides the base from which you grow. With the right strategy, you can build a business with foundations so strong it will last forever.

If you learn and use the 100% Success strategy, you will build a business based on bedrock. This strategy is simple and easy to learn. There is no confusion [which is the enemy of all success in this business.]

You will recognize the concept of 'learn skills first' as the normal practice in all industries in the world and it will give you 100% confidence to make your 100% effort to succeed.

By following 100% Success Basics everyone can succeed.
Even you.

Don't miss the boat

You will love this story…

It had been pouring with rain for days and everyone knew the valley was going to flood. Jim sat in his house and said to himself, 'It will be OK, I've prayed to God and I know he'll send a sign and save me.'

Shortly, there was a knock on the door and Jim opened it to find a policeman. The policeman said, 'Come on, Jim. The dam's busted and the whole valley will be flooded. I've got a truck, let's go!'

Jim smiled and said, 'You go on, I'm OK. I've prayed and I know God will save me.'

Well, the waters came and rapidly flooded the ground floor, so Jim moved to the first floor.

There was a knock on the window, a soldier poked his head in and said, 'Come on Sir, the waters are rising but I'm in a boat, so come on.'

Jim smiled and said 'You go on, I'm OK. I've prayed and I know God will save me.'

Well, the waters kept rising and flooded the first floor so Jim moved on to the roof.

With a thud-thud of rotors, Jim looked up to see a helicopter whose load master called to say, 'Come on Sir, the waters are still rising, we can take you out.'

Jim smiled and said 'You go on, I'm OK. I've prayed and I know God will save me.'

Well, the waters kept rising and so Jim got washed off and drowned.

When Jim arrived in heaven he was furious and stormed up to God and said 'What is the story? I prayed and prayed and what help did you send?'

'What help?' said God. 'What about the policeman, boat and helicopter! What more did you want?'

The Network Marketing industry has evolved and the big Growth boom has arrived.

The two most important developments are a focus on customer development and a new form of **Network System based on the 100% Success strategy.**

Finally the chance of you being successful has dramatically increased.

What will you do with this opportunity?

Will you miss the boat?

CONTENTS

Fundamentals. What a most important word.

Fundamentals. This word calls attention to the primary issue in our quest for greater success. It is the key word in making our lives work well.

Fundamentals. Those 'basics' that build the foundation for accomplishment, productivity, success and lifestyle.

Fundamentals form the beginning, the basis, the reality from which everything else flows. And remember there are no new fundamentals.

Fundamentals are old, well established.

Beware of someone, who claims to have a new fund-amental.

That's like someone who manufactures antiques.

We would have to be suspicious, right?

So Fundamentals. Basics. They are so very important to understand, consider and practice, if you wish for the good life.

And may I add here, make sure you do not look for the exotic answers to success. Success is a very basic process. It doesn't fall out of the sky.

It doesn't have any mysteries. Nor does it fall into the realm of the miraculous.

Success is merely a natural result that comes from the consistent operation of the practical fundamentals. As someone wisely remarked. To be successful you don't have to do extraordinary things, Just do ordinary things extraordinarily well.

Leadership Philosopher, Jim Rohn

Evolution Creates Massive Opportunities

All industries evolve

Who would imagine that in the 1970's the franchising industry was so scorned that the US Congress came within a few votes of outlawing it and the British Government was considering doing the same?

Who would believe that one of the primary reasons that the British Franchising Association was formed in the 1970's was *'To try to disassociate reputable franchisors from pyramid selling operations'*. Yes, it was franchising that was associated with pyramid selling!

In their early days, most franchise companies also used a strategy best described as a **Recruiting Game**.

They focused on just **recruiting** new franchisees, only to then leave them to survive alone whilst they focused on recruiting more new franchisees. The **failure rate was massive.**

All new industries are pioneered by entrepreneurs and have high failure rates. What caused the government and media attacks was that franchising was appealing to risk-averse Entrepreneurs called **(Intrapreneurs)** who were attracted by the claims of 'proven success systems'.

Intrapreneurs created Boom

Following the actions of companies like McDonalds, smart franchising companies evolved their systems to produce very high success rates. This attracted a flood of Intrapreneurs and produced a Growth boom that has lasted over 20 years. The most important innovation was the introduction of **competence based systems.**

Competence based franchise systems detailed exactly WHAT a new franchisee must learn and do. They detailed HOW a franchise should be operated. They introduced Performance STANDARDS. They effectively eliminated the risk of owning a franchise to be able to guarantee success.

With the skyrocketing success of the individual franchisees, there was a new global boom far bigger than the original establishment boom. In the UK, the industry grew by a **staggering 500% in 6 years.** Franchising is now a multi-trillion dollar global industry with an annual failure rate of less than 10%. An amazing success rate considering 40% of businesses normally fail in their first year and 80% in the first 5 years.

NETWORK MARKETING

In the last few decades, the Direct Sales industry has boomed as the Network Marketing business opportunity has driven growth. Over 95% of Direct Sales companies offer Network Leadership opportunities with over **$100 billion in sales operating in more than 100 countries of the world.**

Like franchising before it, Network Marketing has been established using the 'Recruiting Game' strategy, that we call MLM strategy, because we evolved from commission-only direct sales and were established by appealing to entrepreneurs. This naturally produced an unacceptably low success rate and created some concerns in the public as to whether people can succeed in this industry.

Not surprisingly, the most exciting evolution in this industry is the new competence based (100% Success) network systems. Instead of new people focusing on Performance, they are focused on becoming Competent. With Competence comes confidence, increased motivation and thus results.

New Intrapreneur Boom

The new competence first approach had transformed productivity, activity and retention rates which have sky-rocketed incomes and the stability of incomes.

Most importantly, the dramatic increase rates means that the risk-adverse Intrapreneurs are now attracted to this industry en-masse with a new confidence. As a Network Leadership 'Franchise' is more rewarding, flexible and fun than a normal franchise, the industry is expecting the bulk of Intrapreneurs to join it in the future.

This book will explain WHAT you need to learn and do to guarantee success. This 'People's Franchise' is simple for you to understand and you have your sponsor to help you learn.

You can learn more about who this industry is evolving and now enters a 5 year boom and 30 year growth stage by reading Ed's million-selling '100% Confidence' book.

If you learn the 100% Success strategy, the result MUST be 100% Confidence in your products, in your business, in your future. So ask yourself this question…

What would I do if I knew I couldn't fail?

What business is this?

The biggest killer of success in this business is confusion so we will try to ensure that you are 100% clear on everything you need to know.

The first point is over the name of this industry; is it Direct Sales, Network Marketing, MLM, Team Marketing, Direct Marketing or something else?

Point 1. We are in the **Direct Sales** industry.
We sell direct to customers which we get using people that we know. Our competitors are Retail Shops and Direct Marketing companies who get their customers using media such as TV, Radio or Newspapers.

Point 2. The business opportunity is called **Network Marketing**. The name Multi-level marketing or MLM is too often associated to the recruiting pyramids and high failure rate strategies of old that it is not used by mainstream Direct Sales.

In the English speaking world, **Network Marketing** is the most commonly used term by the field network which is why we will use this term for the rest of the book. Frankly, the term you use does not matter as long as we all understand what we are talking about!

The customer is king,
queen and executioner

Lesson One
We Inspire Friends

Your first lesson must be the 'Big Picture' on 'How' and 'Why' Network Marketing works for you. We are in the Sales & Marketing business so what is the strategy?

MARKETING STRATEGY

We market Direct to the customer. To find our customers, we approach people we already know or meet in the normal routine of our daily life. We could call them 'friends'. In the business, they are known as your 'warm market'.

'Friends' is a broad term to mean everyone from your close family to acquaintances, new and old. They form what could be called your 'social network'. Professionals in 'Social Networking' estimate that every adult knows at least 500 people.

We can approach friends because we have a relationship with them. We have an instant introduction and the possibilities to introduce a product or business opportunity under certain conditions. These conditions are discussed under Sales Strategy.

We also market to people we meet in our daily lives; casual encounters. This is why you should always have some marketing tool with you. You may meet them at a supermarket, work, a school function or on holiday. There are opportunities for you to take if you wish.

Most people would meet more than one hundred new people each year in these sorts of circumstances.

Warm Market = Social Network + Casual Encounters

Cold Market

The 'cold market' are people that you have no relationship with. They fall into two categories; people you attract to you through marketing activities or people you approach directly.

You can attract people using marketing activities that your leaders can teach you. You may use these activities after approaching your warm market or in conjunction with your warm market approaches. They should never be instead of warm market approaches as this concept is the core of our business.

We are not in the business of approaching the cold market directly; we do not 'door-knock', 'cold call', use spam emails or any other professional marketing techniques.

SALES STRATEGY

There are two types of 'sales': Professional and Inspirational Sales.

'**Professional Sales**' are used in business and the sales people use professional sales techniques such as 'closing' language, and they will use pressure to get the sale.

'**Inspirational Sales**' are when products are 'soft sold' using only information and inspiration to 'inspire' the person to buy. You still have to answer questions and ask them to buy yet again, no professional sales techniques and certainly NEVER use any pressure.

The Network Marketing business is built using people who will only use Inspirational Sales Techniques and as we market to 'friends' we can only use Inspirational Sales. We talk to people we know, we present the products and through our confidence, inspiring stories and enthusiasm, the person decides whether they want to try the products.

Any techniques required to ensure the person will buy are very basic and able to be learnt by anyone.

GROWTH STRATEGY

The development of a Network Marketing business drives the growth of a company and this process is also controlled by the same conditions as the Sales and Marketing strategies.

We approach people we know with information on our business opportunity. We provide inspiring stories of how the business has been successful to provide confidence in them making a decision. Any techniques required to ensure the person will join are very basic and able to be learnt by anyone.

CONFIDENCE

Many new people are concerned about the concept of 'sales' to the warm market because they do not understand what is required. Once you learn and practice the skills, you will build your confidence and will eventually find it easy to discuss your products and opportunity with anyone.

What you must never do is to focus on the cold market to avoid your warm market. The cold market is the hardest form of sales and you are almost guaranteed to fail. Remember the key is building confidence through practicing skills.

THE BIG POINT

The challenge that people have with this business is the concept of 'Inspirational Sales' to people they know. The fact is that people you know and meet do not mind if you tell them about a product or business IF you do it in a natural, enthusiastic and non-pressured way.

The best mental state is to not care if they act or not. This is the only way to ensure that the person does not feel pressured and for them to be truly inspired by what you are offering. On an emotional level, your eyes will reflect your heart. The person needs to see care in your eyes, not money.

Key Points

This is the basic business model of a Network Marketing business. There is NO other alternative.

- We market to our warm market - Social Network + Casual Encounters

- Eventually we can use marketing techniques whereby people approach us

- We always approach warm markets first

- We only use Inspirational Sales

- We use the same Sales and Marketing to build our businesses as to find customers

*"Confidence is the bridge connecting
expectations and performance,
investment and results"*

RosaBeth Kantor

Lesson Two
Develop 100% Confidence in your Decision

"Whatever the mind of man can conceive and believe,
it can achieve"

Napoleon Hill – Think and Grow Rich

Many people think that success in Network Marketing is based on motivation. Your next lesson in Network Marketing is that success is not about motivation, success is based on CONFIDENCE.

Everyone who joins a Network Marketing business is motivated. In fact, I believe that everyone has a deep well of limitless motivation, normally driven by silently held dreams just waiting to be released. Confidence releases these dreams. **Confidence releases motivation.**

The key to Network Marketing success is action. Only **confidence allows you to act.**

Confidence is the key to successful communication.

We approach people we know with products and the business opportunity.

These people already know us so the communication is much more complex.

The words matter very little, when we talk about products and the business, the other person is really reading our non-verbal communication.They know they may have to 'buy' something so they are looking for one thing in our eyes, voice, facial gestures, body movements... **confidence**.

Remember we do not 'sell' to people we know. We do not put pressure on them. We must inspire them to try our products or join our business. This takes confidence in what you are offering and the enthusiasm it produces.

It is nearly impossible to fake confidence or enthusiasm, to people you know. If they feel that you are trying to fake it, you make them very nervous and they get very sceptical about your products or business.

Confidence in Network Marketing is based on four things:

1. Belief that you have made **a smart decision** to market the products.

2. Belief that you have made **a smart decision** to join the business as it has massive potential. This belief comes from understanding your opportunity.

3. Belief that your **business system will produce success** and that you are able to do it. This belief comes from understanding how the system works.

4. **Competence in skills.** You must prove yourself ABLE to succeed. Until you are competent, you are incompetent! How can you be confident if you are incompetent?

SMART DECISIONS

You will often hear people say that Network Marketing is a 'heart' business. Success comes from the 'heart'. We are an industry of helpers, coaches, advisors and supporters. We are an industry driven by passion, belief, care and inspiration. All this is true YET FIRST you must lead with your head.

SMART DECISION TO MARKET PRODUCTS

95% of people join a Network Marketing business because of the products. They believe that the products are great; they want to use them so others will as well. Is this you?
Great.

If you believe this then it's nearly all you need to believe you have made a smart decision. When you talk to people about your products, just let that confidence and enthusiasm out and people will get the message. No words will ever say more than the excitement in your eyes or in the tone of your voice.

Some people say that Network Marketing is just a system and a connection with the product is not important. It's the old 'Could a vegetarian own a McDonalds beef burger restaurant argument?'

Of course they could, yet would they want to?

And would they be successful?

Would they really be able to communicate a passion for the products to their staff so they in turn could communicate this to their customers?

Of course not.

It's a ridiculous theoretical argument that does not stand up in life. In this business you must feel a connection, an excitement about your products. No passion, no success.

Bit more research

Passion is important, but, if you want 100% confidence that you have made a smart decision to market these products, you need to do a bit more research. Get some facts as to why your products really are great value for the customer.

This does not mean an in-depth analysis. You do NOT need comparisons with other competitor products. You just need a few more facts to build on your belief and marketing story. If it takes more than an hour to listen/learn this research then you are wasting your time!

SMART DECISION TO JOIN BUSINESS

Most people do little research before joining a Network Marketing company and let us be very clear here:

- You have joined a business that will require significant investment of time and effort.

- The rewards are substantial and you could get rich.

- You will be discussing this business with people you know so your decision is being questioned.

Bit more research

Just like with your products, you need to do a bit more research into the WHAT and WHY your opportunity really is such a great business.

To have more confidence.

The basics are in your business presentation. It covered the important points and it has inspired you [or you should not have joined!]

Yet it is not enough.

We are promoting a business here. So just as if we were writing a Business Plan, we need a few more facts on the key parts to the Business Opportunity:

1. What is the opportunity in your <u>Product</u> sector? And how does your company meet this opportunity?

2. What is the opportunity in your <u>Distribution</u> channel for your products? A distribution channel is using shops or selling direct.

3. Why does <u>your company and its business system</u> offer success?

With simple credible answers to these questions, any person should have the confidence that they are 'in the Right Place at the Right Time'.

Your network organisation will provide the required information, my job is to explain WHAT is needed and WHY you must read and understand it!

1. Products Opportunity

You need a clear explanation why the products category your company is in is booming and how they will exploit it. The answers should be simple and obvious.

Get a few facts, some trends and then a clear opinion of what is expected to happen over the next 10 years. All you need is one or two pages of information. Or maybe a CD.

With this knowledge, you will have:

1. 100% confidence that your products have the potential of <u>massive sales</u>

2. A simple explanation to use when discussing your products potential <u>with prospects</u>

3. A simple explanation to use when discussing your products <u>with friends and family.</u> Their support is valuable so you want to be able to show why you are 'smart' to be involved in this boom business area.

> WARNING - Do not get paralysis by analysis! Some people get lost in the product books, CD's or markets. A couple of pages or a CD will do!

2. Distribution Opportunity

This is how you distribute your products to the customer.
Does the customer go to the shop or does the shop go to the customer?
How is the product sold?
How is it delivered?

Network Marketing is in the 'Direct' distribution sector called Direct Sales. In Direct Sales, a person gets the customer.

The other form of Direct distribution is called Direct Marketing which is when a customer is gained through media, such as Internet, newspapers, TV or radio.

Network Marketing has many other names, such as Multi-Level Marketing, MLM, Team marketing and residual marketing. If the growth of a company is driven by an opportunity to create an income based on a multi-leveled network of people then it's 'Network Marketing'.

Why is Direct Selling a boom area?

Direct Selling is a high growth sector of consumer marketing because:
* This is a proactive form of marketing – we go to people rather than wait for them to read a newspaper or go into a shop. This gives us marketing power.

- We can <u>educate</u> the customer. There are so many different products and deals today that customers have become increasingly confused. Confused customers buy from names they trust [known as brands] or from those who educate them.

- We <u>inspire</u> the customer. Our customers try our products based on their potential performance and because we relate our success stories. The presentation is personal and emotional.

The History and Future

It is also vital that you are able to explain a simple history of Network Marketing for them to have confidence in the future.

Read or listen to the **100% Confidence Why Network Marketing is booming again.** An hour invested will have you absolutely convinced about the exciting future of Direct Sales.

3. Company and System

Company

People think they need to learn everything about their company to feel secure. Many companies are huge. Therefore they are large, stable, secure. That's it! If your company is small or new, then simply find out why it has a strong future.

Ask for proof. If you are with a good company, they will provide this proof.

The most important element you will need to communicate is why someone can succeed with your company. This is why a **100% Success** based network system is so important. It will give you the confidence that you need to project to people. Promote it heavily.

Key Points

1. Confidence is the key to success in Network Marketing. It releases motivation. It produces action. It is the key to communication, especially with people you know.

2. Confidence is based on:
   a. Smart decision on products
   b. Smart decision on business
   c. Understanding the system will work for you
   d. Competence in skills

3. A bit more research on why your products are great to market will build confidence in them.

4. A bit more research on why Direct Sales and Network Marketing are the Right Industry at the Right Time will build confidence to promote your business.

"Catch fire with enthusiasm
and people will walk for miles to see you burn."
Reverend Wesley

Lesson Three
Promote Two Great Opportunities

Network Marketing businesses are built by people selecting one of two great opportunities - becoming a Retailer or a Networker.

1. Retailer

a. An opportunity based purely on **making money from getting customers.** Known in business as 'Retail'.

b. Millions of people love the Retail Opportunity for the income potential with flexibility and other benefits such as skills, recognition, new friends and a positive environment.

c. ANYONE can succeed if they learn the skill of Retail.

d. If you stop working then the income stops unless you build a customer base of committed customers, whom we call 'buyers'. (Discussed in later lessons.)

e. Retailers should not recruit people because they do not know how to coach .

f. Retailers provide the **customer power** to a Network Marketing company.

This is a great opportunity and most people in the world of Direct Sales are Retailers.

2. Networker

a. A business opportunity based upon making income from the customer volume of your marketing network.

b. Income is limited only by the size of your network and the customer volume it produces.

c. The income can become residual if customers keep buyers and Networkers become independent.

d. The most important skill is Coaching.

e. Networkers provide the growth and stability in a Network Marketing company.

A 'Networker' is given different names in different companies such as distributor, consultant, associate, representative or IBO. Different names for the same business opportunity. This book deals with how to be successful as a Networker.

Two distinct opportunities
It is important to be clear...

However people may explain your business, it will be based on these two opportunities. This way your business matches the two main groups looking for self-employed opportunities; Part-timer [Retailer] and Intrapreneur [Networker].

See the section on Self-employed Opportunities in the book 100% Confidence by Ed Ludbrook for further explanation.

Understanding the model

There are other types of opportunities in this business that you should be aware of:

1. **Retail Team Leaders.** These people build a team of Retailers and earn commissions. The dominant skills to earn money are sponsoring and coaching of their Retailers so they are actually Networkers building a single level network of Retailers.
Even though their income is limited by the people they can personally manage, they should be encouraged as this is probably the level they feel confident in.

2. **Direct Customer.** Some people get confused and include customers who buy directly from the company as being part of their 'Network'. Customers buy your product for its value alone, do not include them in any business discussion.

Workers not Talkers

When looking at opportunities in our business it is very important to understand the difference between dreams and action. This is especially true of a Network opportunity as the joining cost is so low.

When you compare the two opportunities, some Networkers will see the opportunity to earn a big residual income thus they wonder 'Why would anyone want to be a Retailer?'

The first point is that there are lots of people who just enjoy talking about and promoting products or they want to make a small amount of money for a specific reason and thus Retailer opportunity is perfect for them. They are not interested in a business [no matter how you paint the story].

The second point is that whilst many people may be excited about a big residual income yet are they prepared to work for this? Are they workers or talkers? If you sponsor someone who is a 'talker' rather than 'a worker', they will cost you time, effort and money!

Retailer-Networker Ratio

A question many people ask is whether there is a correct ratio between Retailers and Networkers? That is, should you have three Retailers to every Networker or should it be five?

There is no correct answer YET you should remember that there will always be more people prepared to work to make money from Retailing than will be prepared to work to build a network.

WHY DO PEOPLE BECOME RETAILERS?

The reason is Lifestyle money!

New Networkers also are inspired about this financial opportunity.

The power of Network Marketing is that it can improve your Lifestyle by increasing your Lifestyle Money, commonly known as **Disposable Income**.

AFTER-TAX INCOME	
Less	Mortgage, insurance, car payments, pension, commitments
Less	vital shopping
Equals	DISPOSABLE INCOME

Most people would admit that over 90% of their income is spent on vital expenses (maybe 100% is too low!)

So let's assume an average household after-tax income of approx. $3,000 per month so the average household has only **$300 per month in disposable income** (i.e. 10% of $3,000)

Networking's power is that it can earn anyone at least $300 per month profit in less than three months (some in less than one month). That means Network Marketing can **double the lifestyle of the average household.** Governments should make Network Marketing compulsory!

Sponsoring Tip

This 'double your lifestyle' approach to sponsor new retailers is very effective.

Key Points
To understand Network Marketing, we need to remember that:
- There are two distinct opportunities: Retailer and Networker
- The two opportunities work in harmony
- The two opportunities match the main groups of people looking for self-employed opportunities
- Whilst people may 'talk' of working to be a Network business, you should only deal with 'workers'.
- There will always be more people prepared to join as Retailers than Networkers.

100% ACTION

Review this section so you understand the basic concept and then review your business to ensure you are clear on the opportunities you offer and the sort of people who will take them.

Lesson Four
Anyone can get Rich

So who wants to get rich? What a question!

In reality, most people hate talking about money yet the concept of 'being rich' has enchanted people since the dawn of time.

Yet you need to think about **'what does rich mean?'**

We believe that **'Rich'** is not an amount of money, being **'Rich'** is a feeling.

Getting 'rich' is not what most people imagine. It's not about Ferraris and helicopters.

Famous leadership expert Dr Stephen Covey studied the literature written by people when they knew they were going to die. What do you think they wrote about?
Wished they spent more time at work?
Lived in a bigger house?
Drove better cars?
More adventure?

No, all they wrote about was their relationships. Their good relationships. Their poor relationships. True happiness is in the relationships we have. Our relationships make us Rich.

Relationships are the basis of truly being rich.

For the average person, getting rich means an absence of financial worries and the time to invest in their relationships. Money and time freedom. A feeling of security, and happiness.

The reality of life is that we need money and most people struggle investing time and energy into relationships because they have to make money.

This means that to 'Be Rich' we need to not worry about earning enough money to satisfy our needs each month and have the time freedom to enjoy it. To be able to develop relationships.

Think of those books and movies about the rich yet **lonely** man. No-one wishes to have his life for all the money in his bank account.

For the average person, they don't need to earn 'millions'. Most people need a '**management level**' income to feel rich.

Approx $100,000 per year.

Also note that due to the taxation benefit's of a home-based business, a $100,000 income from a Network Marketing business with the added incentives such as travel, is probably equivalent to a **$150,000 income** from a job or business.

It is not just the amount that is important, the income must be secure. It must be what is called **Residual**.

Residual means that you wake up on the 1st of every month, knowing that money is paid into your bank account whether you work or not! Heaven.

TO FEEL RICH MOST PEOPLE NEED TO EARN A $100,000 PER YEAR RESIDUAL

With money and freedom, you have the choices to develop those relationships. Also you can develop your other passions; such as sports, hobbies, adventure or service to others.

When you add the flexibility of work times, home-based environment, the travel, new confidence and endless new relationships, maybe, you could believe that this is the Greatest Opportunity in the World.

$100,000 PER YEAR IN NETWORK MARKETING?

How possible is it to earn $100,000 per year in Network Marketing?

If you learn and work the 100% Success Strategy, I believe it is guaranteed. [Well nearly guaranteed.] In this book, you will be shown the exact strategies required to make $100,000 per year.

WHEN $100,000 = $1,000,000

To get you really motivated, you should appreciate that what you will be creating is Residual Income. Residual means a $100,000 per year income that lasts.

IF you build your network correctly based on the 100% Success strategy with a good company, it should last a long time. Ten years is not unreasonable. I know of some incomes that are still paying strongly after 10 years. Do the calculations - $100,000 per year x 10 years = $1,000,000.

Are you prepared to learn
and work hard for two years for $1,000,000?

WANT TO EARN MORE?

No problem.

If you get to $100,000 per year then $1,000,000 per year is achievable through the application of the same strategy but just operating a lot more aggressively for longer.

Anyone CAN earn $100,000 per year in Network Marketing if you follow the 100% Success strategy

Key Points

- Getting Rich is a Feeling.

- For most people to 'Get Rich' they need to earn a residual 'management level' income of approx $100,000. The lack of stress and time freedom allows them to develop better relationships and lifestyle.

- Anyone CAN earn $100,000 per year in Network Marketing if you follow the 100% Success strategy.

- $100,000 per year residual is really $1,000,000 if you build it correctly.

- If you can make $100,000 per year, $1,000,000 is possible with the same skills, just more effort.

Lesson Five
Leadership Income Takes
Two Steps

To achieve a Residual income of $100,000 per year to 'Feel Rich', first you must get to a **Leadership Rank** and then turn your earnings into **Leadership Income**.

Step 1 - Leadership Rank

As the network model is based on earning a little bit of money from a lot of people, achieving this requires that you have 'a lot' of people. You need Numbers. The positions where you have enough people for a 'management level' income are called LEADER ranks. This is achieved by:

1. Working your **Network system**

2. **Creating Momentum** using the TidalWave [Lesson 13]

Big Money

Leadership Rank

Builder

Join

YOUR FIRST GOAL IS TO BECOME A LEADER

Builder

Until you reach Leader Rank, your job is to 'build the network' so you are called a BUILDER. Do not expect to make an interesting income as a Builder because you do not have enough people yet.

When you reach the LEADER Rank, you must then learn further leadership skills. They are taught to you on achieving this Rank.

Big Money

The big money is at the higher Leader ranks. They have titles such as Diamond, 5 Star or SpaceShip Commander! [Just joking].

If you can become a 'Leader', then you have proven you have what it takes to achieve any higher rank. You will then be taught what is required to become a Diamond! Achievement is then based on effort and time.

Step 2 - Leadership Income

Creating Momentum will give you the numbers to have a Leadership Rank, yet it will not give you a Leadership Income that is stable and residual. This is because to create momentum you will naturally over emphasise sponsoring people rather than building customer volume and learning skills.

By everyone working your Network system, they will naturally produce some customer volume and learn some level of skills. Once you have achieved Leadership Rank, you must then focus on developing sufficient customer volume and skill levels.

Three Elements of Network Success

Your network requires three important elements.

They are:

1. Number of Networkers

2. Customer volume

3. Competence = the number of Independent Retailers and Networkers. Competence comes from learning skills.

A weakness in any of the three elements will mean your Residual income will not last. The common mistakes are:

1. All numbers. This is the classic *MLM* error where all focus is placed on recruitment and nothing on customers or competence. No customer volume or low competence levels produces low incomes and low confidence. The result is Builders stop building a network. It's like building houses on sand.

2. All customers. A network that focuses too much on customers does not produce the fast growth needed to develop exciting Builder incomes. The result is growth stops.

3. No competence. A network focused solely on numbers and customers sometimes ignores competence development and so creates no independent people. Results are created yet no clarity of performance or independence is produced so eventually it causes problems.

How long does it take?

Using the Tidalwave strategy, it takes approximately 12 months to create momentum and reach a Leadership Rank. Then it should take a further 12 months to ensure that there is sufficient customer volume and competence in your network to create **Leadership Income**. Some people will do it faster, others slower.

Two years on average to create an income to be 'rich'. Most people never have this in 40 years of work!

Key Points

1. There are two distinct opportunities – Retailer and Networker.

2. The goal of being a Networker is to become a Leader.

3. When a Networker has not achieved a Leader Rank, they are called a Builder.

4. You achieve the Leader Rank through momentum using the TidalWave strategy. Explained later.

5. Once you are at Leader Rank, you need to focus on customer volume and competence to create a residual Leadership Income.

6. It takes approximately 12 months to achieve a Leadership Rank using the TidalWave strategy to create momentum and a further 12 months to create Leadership Income.

Lesson Six
Build Maximum
Customer Volume

Creating customer volume is one of the three elements to creating a successful network marketing business. Customer volume is the total of the purchases made with the company in your personal group. It comes from three sources:

1. Your personal usage

2. Your personal customers

3. Retailers

1. Personal Usage

Personal usage is all the orders you place for personal use. Obviously, you should be using as many of your company's products as you can. If possible, set up an autoshipping programme to make sure you get these products regularly.

Using the products is important because you market products not by employing professional sales techniques, but through inspirational selling. No pressure, just great products and positive testimonials about the quality of the product.

2. Personal Customers

Personal customers either buy from you or direct from the company. They have not joined the business and just want to enjoy your products.

You get customers by using the skill of RETAIL. It does not matter whether you want to be a middle rank Leader or the Global No1, you must have personal customers. The correct strategy is as follows:

- Build a base first. Everyone must get an initial number of customers as fast as possible. You should plan to get these initial customers in the first week from people you know.

- Get competent. Focus on learning the Retail skill until you have passed the competence standard [explained later]. Your system will explain what the Retail Competence Standard is.

- Regular results. Once you are competent, you will naturally get customers on a regular basis.

3. Retailers

Some people who join your business will just want the Retailer opportunity which is solely focused on getting customers for money. Excellent! They have a huge impact on Customer Volume. Where your personal consumption and customers add hundreds to your volume, Retailers add thousands. Multiply this volume by lots of Builders and numbers get exciting!

Your job as a sponsor of a Retailer is to Coach them, to help them learn the skill of RETAIL. Their job is the other two sources of customer success - Personal Consumption and Personal Customers.

Success Tip – Make Money Forever

Retailers naturally have lower goals and have a shorter term focus. They want to make cash fast which is great. The challenge is that they focus on results when they are not competent [ie incompetent] at the skill. This destroys their confidence and they quit.

Explain to all new Retailers that they should focus on becoming competent first. It still means they will be producing results and making money [probably more money]. More importantly, they will eventually become competent and will always be able to make money with your company. They will be able to MAKE MONEY FOREVER.

The importance of Customer Volume

It is natural for a Builder to focus almost entirely on sponsoring other Builders and encouraging them to do the same. The only volume is Personal Consumption.

Without customers, there is not enough volume for the majority of Builders to make enough income so they eventually stop working. Networks built on this strategy always collapse.

It sounds like a smart idea but ignoring customer volume is a major mistake and always results in failure [strong enough warning for you?]

Key Points

• Customer volume comes from three areas.

• Personal consumption is vital. Take an autoship.

• Personal customers are obtained by the skill of Retail. Learn until you are competent.

• Retailers focus just on customers. They should also focus on competence.

• Be warned that no customer volume = no long term success.

100% ACTION

Now is a good time to discuss what you would expect your Customer Volume to be. Discuss this with your sponsor. You want to understand what you should expect to produce and thus what you expect other Networkers to produce.

Lesson Seven
Sponsor and Harness the Power of Duplication

Anyone can achieve a Leadership Rank because they do not have to sponsor huge numbers of people. The numbers are created by sponsoring a few then tapping into the Exponential Power of Numbers, or the **Power of Duplication**.

WHAT IS THE POWER OF DUPLICATION?

The following question and answer reveals its power... *Would you want $100,000 cash today or 1 cent doubled every day for 30 days?"*

$100,000 sounds fantastic yet the power of duplication will turn that cent into a fortune.

- On day 1, you have 1c.
- On day 2, you have 2c (1c doubled).
- Day 3, you have 4c (2c doubled).
- By day 10, you only have $5.12...
- By day 20, you have $5,242.88, and...
- On day 25 you overtake the $100,000 mark with $167,772.16...
- But by day 30, you would receive $5,368,709.12

HOW DO WE USE THE POWER OF DUPLICATION?

The power of networking comes from the people. It is about a lot of people creating a little volume not a few people creating a lot of volume. So you **must create 'a lot of people'**.

You get a lot of people using the Power of Duplication. By just sponsoring two Builders and getting them to do the same and so on, you could earn an income from 62 Builders' volume.

You introduce 2 Builders

2 introduces	2 each	= 4
4 introduces	2 each	= 8
8 introduces	2 each	= 16
16 introduces	2 each	= 32
	Total	= 62

Builders

This is the concept of **Leverage**.

Creating leverage means you are amplifying a small effort to create a large result. The Power of Duplication is the force that amplifies your efforts.

The Power of Duplication means everyone can create large numbers in their Network.

INCREASE THE LEVERAGE

If you only earned $1 from every person every month, it is not a lot of money. Yet use Leverage to introduce more earning power.

More levels

On your 5th level there are 32 people. IF you added ONE MORE LEVEL and earned down to your 6th level, the total numbers would be **126 people. 100% increase.**

More width

Adding width is much more powerful than adding levels. Instead of using a sponsoring multiple of 2, what about using 3? IF everyone added one more each, then the total number of Builders jumps to 363! You still only introduced three personally.

> You introduce 3
> 9
> 27
> 81
> 243
> Total = 363 Builders

Just one more EACH adds 301 people [363-62]. Adding just one more wide produces a **500% Increase.**

If it was five instead of two, the total is 3,905! **6000% increase.**

**Lesson - Sponsoring more people dramatically
increases your potential income**

More customer volume

From the above examples, if you only earned $1 per month per Builder it would be a nice small income, wouldn't it? Remember you personally only sponsored a few Builders!

Yet $1 per month is not right. As I explained in previous chapters, customer volume is critical to success so it's more accurate to multiply by $5 or more. Now the income is in the thousands and gets exciting!

Not only could you take a $1,000 per month income to $5,000, it builds strength and security into your network.

Key Points

1. By sponsoring just a few Builders into your business and harnessing the Power of Duplication can give you a group in the hundreds or thousands.

2. By sponsoring more Builders, the power of Duplication dramatically increases the Numbers.

3. Increased customer volume dramatically increases your income and builds strength and security

---

Lesson Eight
Learn Skills FIRST

Using the Power of Duplication to build a network is not revolutionary. I am sure you were introduced to the concept to explain why Networking has such power. The key is to understand how this works in practice and discover the power of the 100% Success Strategy.

So let's look at the theory.

You –		Retail
3	–	Sponsor
9	–	Coach
27	–	Coach
81	–	Coach

It starts with YOU.
What do you do?

To create Customer Volume, you use the products and find your own Personal Customers. You achieve this with the SKILL of Retail.

To find new Retailers and Builders, you use the SKILL of Sponsoring, sometimes known as Recruiting.

Then you need your Retailers to LEARN the skill of Retail and your Builders to LEARN the skills of Retail and Sponsoring. The skill of HELPING people LEARN is called the skill of COACHING.

So the **three key skills** of a **Network Marketing business** are:
- Retail – the skill of building a customer base
- Sponsor – the skill of introducing new Retailers and Builders
- Coach – the skill of helping people learn the skills of Retail, Sponsor and Coach.

Success Tip – It is vital that you use the correct terms as the language you use determines the behaviour of your people. The correct term is COACH, not TEACH or TRAIN.

'Teach' or 'train' infers that **you have the responsibility** for their learning. Thus if they do not learn and quit then it's your responsibility; you 'failed' as a teacher or trainer. This is a self-employed opportunity so it is **the Networker's responsibility** to learn the skills. As their sponsor, your job is to HELP THEM LEARN. They learn, you coach. Got it?

THE SYSTEM IS THE SOLUTION

These three skills are the core of your Network System that everyone learns and works. You can see that if everyone works the three skills then the Retail would produce customer volume and the Sponsor and Coaching would produce duplication.

Thus success in Network Marketing is based on **duplicating the system which has three key skills.**

> **Get your language right!**
> People do not 'copy you' or 'duplicate you'. They **learn and work the system** and this creates duplication.
> Only systems can be duplicated.
> We see this in business all of the time. The McDonalds system is the key to their global success. Same with Body Shop. Same with Starbucks.

The information in the system is clear and detailed so there is **no confusion.** Confusion is the cancer of Networking.

A business based on a system means that people can be working if you want to stop. It means that people can be working in other cities, countries and languages; everyone can succeed because everyone is working the same system based on three key skills!

THE SUCCESS SECRET

The key to success is that everyone who joins your network has the responsibility to learn the three skills of the system until they are COMPETENT.

The more competent they are, the more CONFIDENT they become. **Increased confidence = increased results.**

When they are 100% competent, they will be 100% CONFIDENT. Then they will be INDEPENDENT. [How can you be independent if you are still **incompetent?**]

REMEMBER. Independent Retailers and Builders are the key to success. Independent people will work on their own allowing you to develop more people.

They will work on their own allowing you to slow down or stop working. Independent people are the base of all residual incomes.

100% SUCCESS IN NETWORK MARKETING

When people join they **focus on learning** skills until competent, not creating results. The key strategy is to LEARN SKILLS FIRST.
If everyone learns skills then everyone can be successful, ie. 100% Success.

The Recruiting Game strategy sends an incompetent person out to talk to people with the expectation of creating consistent results. Crazy!

Is this strategy unusual?

Of course not!

This is how you learn skills in every job, sport and role in life.

How do you learn the skills?

This is covered in Lessons 10 and 11.

Basically the knowledge will be in your system manuals, you are coached by your sponsor and upline and you learn the skills through practice. **Practice makes perfect.**

Sponsor's sponsor | Sponsor | You | Your frontline

Your upline | Your downline

What is the job of your Sponsor?

They are your COACH.

They are paid commissions on the volume in your network to help you learn the skills until you are competent and confident.

They are NOT paid to sponsor you; this is the technical definition of pyramid selling. Sponsoring someone creates the opportunity to make money from the customer volume their network creates.

They are paid for Coaching.
When does your Sponsor's job finish?

When you are working on your own and PROVEN competent [see Lesson 9 - Become competent], then your sponsor's job is complete.

What is the job of your Upline?
Your upline are those leaders who will earn from the volume your network creates. They are paid those commissions to help your Sponsor coach you. They are your team of Success Coaches.

PURE GENIUS

This Coaching Support System is one of the Genius Elements of Network Marketing and makes it unique in the world of business. In most businesses, the most successful people do not try to make the new people better than they are!

No blame

People with an honest heart will always concern themselves about the potential success of the people they introduce.

If people are working with a 'learn skills first' 100% Success strategy, they have total confidence that the person can succeed if that person wants to.

The only time a person 'fails' is when they stop trying to learn. When they clearly understand that success is based on learning skills and then they can decide to stop, they cannot blame you, your company or Network Marketing for their lack of results!

Key Points
- The system has three key skills: Retail, Sponsor, Coach.
- Numbers are created by everyone learning and working the Network System.
- You learn the skills until you are competent.
- As you build competence, you build confidence. The more competent they become, the more confident they become, the better results they will produce.
- When you are 100% competent and confident, you will be independent which is the basis of a residual income and success in Network Marketing.
- Learn skills through knowledge, coaching and practice.
- Your sponsor is your coach.
- Your upline are success coaches.

The Ultimate Sponsoring Tool

We started this workbook with an example of the question I ask everywhere in the world; How many people could you sponsor if you knew they could not fail?

The answer is always a huge laugh and something like 'everyone!'

When you realize that everyone can succeed because everyone can eventually learn the three skills of a Network System. This means everyone can succeed in Network Marketing.

Promoting guaranteed success is the
Ultimate Sponsoring Tool!

With this confidence in your heart, when you are trying to sponsor someone, now you can look them in the eye and say...

'I know you can succeed because we have a system based on skills that you can learn. Our team will *coach* you until you have learnt the skills and become confident'

SPONSORS AGREEMENT

With each new person [and your sponsor], you should explain the following agreement:

1. You can succeed because you have a system that you can learn.
2. You learn the system until you are 100% competent.
3. You will learn by practice in workshops and with prospects.
4. The sponsor's job is to be the coach and help you learn.
5. Their job is complete when you are competent. They will invest their time in you as long as you are learning.
6. To help the sponsor, you have a team of Success Coaches called your Upline. Their time is valuable.
7. You will learn at your own speed yet will go as fast as you can.

100% SUCCESS
FREQUENTLY ASKED QUESTIONS

Who do I practice on?

- The first person to practice with is your sponsor.

- You can practice with other Networkers in role-play and workshops.

- You 'practice' with prospective customers and Net-workers until you are competent. You may produce fantastic results yet it is still practice!

The best people to 'practice on' are **people you already know.** Friends should naturally be enthusiastic about your products and the potential of the business if you are. They will naturally help you if you are honest in your communication.

This last point is important to understand. When you talk to people, your focus is not creating results, it is **learning through practice.** If you do not get the results you wanted, it does not matter, **AS YOU WERE ONLY PRACTICING.**

Can everyone learn the three skills?

Of course!

The only reason people are not confident in their ability to learn these skills, is because they are not competent yet. Remember Retail and Sponsoring is not based on becoming a super-promoter, success is based on confidence and enthusiasm. These come with practicing the skills.

How much money are you making?

What do you say if someone asks you 'how much money are you making?'

The simple honest reply is something like 'I am making some [or no] money yet as I am just learning'.

Anyone who then scorns you or your income when you are learning is an idiot.

What about my Goals?

When you join it is natural and important to have dreams of success and goals to achieve this success. These goals will be based on earning money, buying things, achieving Leadership Ranks in your compensation plan and earning incentives. These are called **Results Goals**.

These are important yet NOT as important as **Learning and Activity Goals**.

How can you expect to achieve Results Goals when you are still incompetent in the key skills? All results goals are possible yet should be focused on AFTER becoming competent.

LEARNING AND ACTIVITY GOALS FIRST

How long will it take for you to learn the skills? Who knows? This is up to you. Everyone learns at their own pace and in their own way. The more you practice, the faster you will learn.

Does this strategy produce slow results?

Some people will worry that focusing on learning skills before results will produce slower growth and smaller results. They worry that people will 'waste time' in learning when they should be out working. These people have a Recruiting Game mentality.

If someone joins your Network and talks enthusiastically to people they meet, they will create some results.

The other reality is that very quickly, they will do or say the wrong things, discover questions they don't know the answer to, so feelings of incompetence will undermine their confidence. This will reduce their motivation.

They will come back to you and all you can do is give them some more information and 'try to motivate' them more. Yet they will eventually stop working because you are expecting an incompetent person to create satisfactory results.

Fast initial results

The person focused on learning will feel less pressure. They should be more relaxed and communicate more confidence. They will have less fear so will talk to more people. They will naturally produce more results faster. As they are focused on learning they will feel less rejection, they will work longer and so produce more results. A focus on **learning skills first** will produce faster and more consistent results over the long term.

100% ACTION

This is one of the most important lessons. It is vital that you reread this Lesson so you clearly understand it.

Lesson Nine
Become Competent

You build competence into your system because it is:
- the key to productivity [how much people produce]

- the key to long term confidence [how long they produce]

What is competence?
Competence means *'an ability to perform a skill to a certain performance standard'*.

How do I know I am competent?
Just like learning to drive, you must pass a knowledge test [yes, I said test] and achieve a performance standard, called a Competence Standard. Your sponsor will help you test yourself.

What is a Competence Standard?
Unlike a goal, a competence standard is not a one-off target. It is something that you can maintain on your own (so you know it was not a fluke!) Without a standard, how do you know you are competent? An example in Network Marketing terms would be *'to be able to sponsor one new Networker per week for four consecutive weeks.'*

This does not mean four Networkers in the first week. It is the ability to consistently deliver results that counts.

What do I do when I am proven competent?

Have a massive party!

You now have proved that you can be successful in Network Marketing and thus with time and effort, you are guaranteed to achieve a Leadership Income!

What do I learn?

Each skill has required knowledge, skills and attitudes.

* **Knowledge**   = what you need to know

* **Skills**   = what you need to do

* **Attitudes**   = how you need to think

Let's look at the skills of Sponsoring. To master this skill, you must know areas such as …

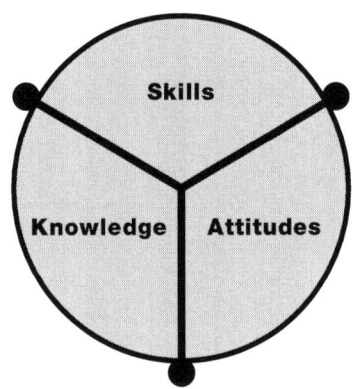

* **Knowledge** – the key points to the opportunity presentation and frequently asked questions;

* **Sub-skills** – each skill is broken into sub-skills that you must master

* **Attitudes** – be enthusiastic, be quick, ask everyone, do not prejudge prospects.

UNDERSTANDING SUB-SKILLS - THE FLYWHEEL

The Sponsoring process is like a Flywheel. The main skill called Sponsoring with four sub-skills which are all connected. If you are shown a different sponsoring process with three or five sub-skills, it does not matter, the theory is effectively the same.

Creating duplication is based on the turning of the Flywheel. If it turns slowly then growth will be slow. If it turns quickly then your network will grow quickly. Getting it turning quickly is covered in the Lesson on the TidalWave. For now, let's look at the theory.

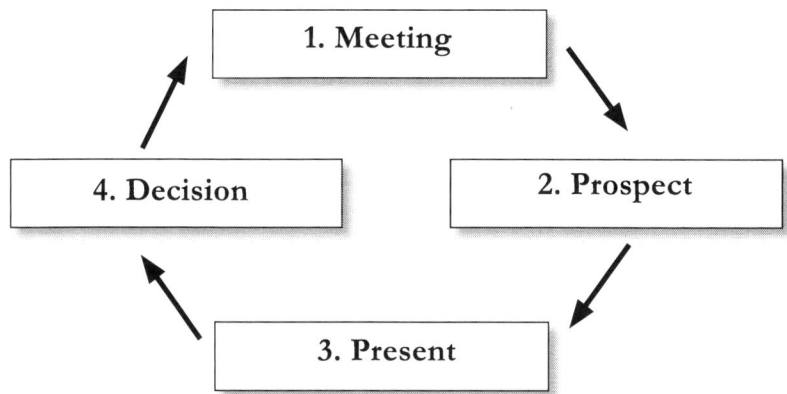

Step 1 - **Meeting**. Someone joins your team. Now for the initial Coaching Session. It is often called something like 'Quick Start', 'Fast Start' or 1st Step training/meeting. In the meeting you will cover subjects such as basic administration, knowledge and skills to get you prospecting, your 'story', goals [especially Learning and Activity Goals], contact list and coming to events.

Step 2 - **Prospect**. Talking to people, to find those who want to hear a product or business presentation. As many as possible. As quickly as possible. Enthusiasm is the key. Your sponsor should help you.

Step 3 - **Present**. Make business presentations to prospects. The more presentations you do, the more people will join.

Step 4 - **Decision**. Answer questions. Ask people to join. Follow up on those that are not ready. Some will join and some will not.

For those who join, help them start the cycle at Step One.

Competence in Sponsoring

You need to become competent at each sub-skill to become competent at the main skill of Sponsoring.

Think about it?

You can be excellent at prospecting, presenting and running a first meeting yet if you cannot help people make a decision to join [step 4], you will never be competent at Sponsoring. When you have mastered this sub-skill, you will be able to sponsor.

If you were coaching this person, you would not focus any time on the three sub-skills they can do and instead should focus all your time on helping them learn Step 4: how to get someone to make a decision.

System is detailed

Where do you find out about the knowledge, skills and attitudes you need to learn?

Everything you need to know will be explained in your system. Ask your sponsor for this information if you don't have it.

Just understanding WHAT you need to learn will immediately give you more confidence. It will eliminate any confusion you have. If you are concerned that you cannot do this skill, your lack of confidence is only because you are not competent yet.

Other information
You may have read books, listened to speakers or heard other ideas, tips or techniques on how to perform these skills. IGNORE them. No matter how good you think they are, they will only create confusion in your mind.

The best networkers in your business with your products in your market have developed your system and they know best. The greatest threat to success in Network Marketing is confusion and the introduction of ideas from outside your system is the best way to create confusion.

Key Points

- Competence is the ability to perform a skill to a set performance standard

- Skills are based on attitudes, knowledge and sub-skills

- You prove your competence by passing a knowledge test and achieving a competence standard

- All the knowledge you need is detailed in your Network system

- Ignore any ideas, tips or techniques outside your Network system

- Coaches help you understand and learn your Network system

- Achievement on your compensation plan is not important until you are competent

All important Summary

Now is the time for a quick summary of the 100% Success concept.

1. 100% Success is a simple strategy to get you from joining to a position where your <u>success in Network Marketing is guaranteed</u>. It does not mean you are going to be a superstar. It does not even mean you will succeed as you still need to work to achieve.

2. Guaranteed success comes from becoming <u>competent in the three key skills</u> of your Network System.

3. You can become competent because our business model does not rely on your being a Super-sales person or a Super-Recruiter! It relies on people being able to get a <u>few customers, retailers and networkers</u> on a regular basis. Then working with them correctly so some of those people become 'Buyer' customers, independent Retailers and independent Networkers. The point here is regular activity over a period of time.

4. You know you are competent when you <u>pass the knowledge test and achieve the competence performance standards.</u> The other results you achieve like income, network size, rank, etc are not actually relevant at this stage.

5. If an acceptable number of networkers with Customer Volume keep working then the Power of Numbers will create the opportunity for everyone to achieve/earn exciting incomes. The key then is momentum, covered in Lesson 12.

100% ACTION

Discover from your upline what the competence standards are for your system for each of the skills.

Ask them whether there is a test for the knowledge aspect of your system. If there is no test, ask your upline to create one for you.

The concept of competence is simple to understand if you relate it to normal life such as learning to drive.

LESSON NINE

*"Learning is defined as a change in behaviour.
You haven't learnt a thing until you can
take action and use it."*
Don Shula and Ken Blanchard

Lesson Ten
Accelerate your learning

You become competent by LEARNING. Enjoy this new concept as it can help you in many areas of your life. There are important points you need to keep in mind.

- **This is your career.** There will be no one forcing you to work; you have to want to work.

- **This is not a race.** Everyone will move at different speeds; do not compare your results against those of others.

- **You need to be tested** so you know that you are competent.

- You **cannot expect consistent results until you are completely competent** so do not despair if you do not win all of the time. Mistakes are a part of the learning process.

Everyone learns at different speeds

You learn skills through:
- Learning the knowledge in your Network system.
- Coaching from your sponsor and upline.
- Practicing through 'Role-play' with your sponsor or in groups at a Workshop.
- Practicing on people from your contact list.

Knowledge

All the knowledge/information you need is provided by your network. Be very clear about what has to be learnt. Pass the test. The only acceptable score is 100%.

Coaching

Every discussion with your sponsor and upline is called a Coaching Session. Their job is to coach you until you are competent. They want you to become competent as soon as possible. They will provide Explanation, Demonstration and Feedback. They will help you with your motivation and confidence.

Role-play and workshops

The best 'practice' will always be with actual prospects, yet to improve performance and build confidence, role-playing with your sponsor or other builders is fantastic learning.

Workshops are groups of Builders and Retailers doing role-play. Workshops are a fantastic learning environment. You should attend as many as you can. Keep going back as often as you need to as every workshop will be a different experience, and you will learn something new.

Practice

If you approach talking to prospect customers or Networkers as 'practice' then you will lose the fear of failure. This is why practicing initially with people you know is the best idea, they will help you and not judge you as you are just learning. The more you practice the better you will become.

THE LEARNING PROCESS

Remember when you learned to do something like riding a bike or driving a car? At first it was incredibly awkward but you kept practising and eventually you could do it without even thinking about it.

Step 1 Unconsciously incompetent.

Most people have no idea how to build a Team. You may have some ideas but you actually don't know.

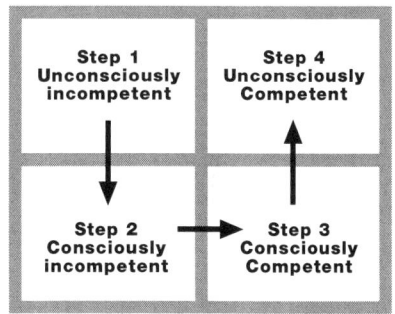

Step 2 Consciously incompetent.

You start and suddenly you find out all the things that you didn't know you had to do.

You make mistakes, say silly things and have minor failures.

You will not learn as fast as you expect and you might not get the results as fast as you expected.

Your upline should coach and test you, just like a driving instructor would.

Step 3 Consciously competent.

You've passed your Coaching Test and you're competent. There will be no more testing but you still need support and experience which your upline and the company provides.

Step 4 Unconsciously competent.

You are a master and will quickly move up your Compensation Plan. You will be confident, gain respect and be on your way to leadership and high incomes.

It will help you greatly if you discuss this learning cycle with every new person you recruit. It clearly puts the whole learning process in context and makes them relax about those initial mistakes.

THE THREE P'S

Success in learning is based on the Three P's:
Practice
You learn all skills through proactive trial and error.
Patience
It always takes time to learn.
Perseverance
You must try, try and try again for success.

Lesson Eleven

The Coaching Session is EVERYTHING

By now you should understand that the 100% Success strategy is based on learning skills and building confidence. Now its time to look at how this strategy works in practice and how you can create the fastest growth possible.

Before we start, you must understand the following three points:

1.   Success is Leadership Income

As we explained in Lesson Five, if you join as a Networker then for you to get an acceptable Return on your Investment of time, effort and money, you must achieve a Leadership Rank with the income to match this position. This is 'success' in Network Marketing. Everything we recommend is targeted at achieving 'success'.

We know that many people join without the confidence to believe they can achieve these 'leadership' positions. Remember this is only a lack of confidence that we can overcome with learning skills and coaching.

2.   The two types of people

It is absolutely critical that you understand the following to succeed in Network Marketing. First, let me ask you a question...

**If 100 people joined your team, how many of them
do you think would be able to master the skills
on their own?**

'On their own' means that whilst they had access to group training and some upline support, all the information and inspirational events, conference calls, etc. they did not however receive personalized competence based coaching.

Research with 1000's of experienced Networkers globally shows that the main range of answers is between 1% and 5%, with the median being 2%.

Yes, just 2 out of every 100 people can become independent on their own!

> The point you MUST accept from this fact is that
> the remaining 98% need EFFECTIVE INDIVIDUAL
> COACHING to learn the core skills and build their
> confidence or they will fail!

And if most of those 98%ers fail then the Network Marketing model does not work very well! Remember, you 'earn a little bit from a lot of people'.

3.   The right type of coaching

It is important to realise that there are TWO types of coaching - Competence and Performance.

Performance Coaching

When most people think of 'coaching', they think of Performance Coaching.

This skill is helping an individual, team or organization succeed through a focus on performance. Through the achievement of Performance Goals. Through better skills tactics, attitude, motivation and other personal development subjects. Most sports, business and life coaching is Performance Coaching.

Competence Coaching

Competence coaching is a similar yet a fundamentally different form of coaching. It is used when the individual can and should focus on learning set skills to a competence standard **BEFORE** focusing on performance.

It allows for the mass standardization of learning performance and guarantees minimum levels of success. You can only use this form of coaching when the skills for success can be learnt to a certain 'competence standard'.

Competence coaching focuses on **Learning and the achievement of Learning Goals**. It is commonplace everywhere if you think about it; schools, companies, professions, the military and government, all coach for competence BEFORE performance.

100% Success Coaching

The classic mistake that people make in Network Marketing is to use Performance Coaching and focus their people of achieving Performance Goals; how much money to make, achieving incentives or a compensation plan rank.

When you think about it, this is like getting a new driver to focus on speed driving before they learn how to drive!

I just want to be clear that when you join this business, you need to write these Performance Goals as they provide inspiration and a focus for achievement ONCE you have built competence.

The reality is that few new people are truly inspired by their Performance Goals or their BIG Dreams.The reason is simply that they fear failure.

The most famous question to discover your true motivations is *'what would you do if you KNEW you could not fail?'* The key words are *'...knew you could not fail'*. Yes, fear of failure is the major reason that holds people back from dreaming their dreams. We know that you can achieve Learning and Activity Goals which why we want you to focus on them to become competent!

The three core skills of Network Marketing are clear and the competence standard can be achieved by anyone, thus **Competence Coaching is the correct form.**

The challenge is that the Network Marketing business is an unique environment and thus the competence coaching required has a specific unique process to follow. We call this form **100% Success Coaching because it produces a 100% chance of success!**

The Coaching Session!

The key to this whole 100% Success coaching and success overall is the 'coaching session'.

The best way to learn skills is to attend 'coaching sessions' run by your upline. Your job as a sponsor or upline is to run 'coaching sessions'. EVERYTHING in building a network is based on a 'coaching session'.

The logic is simple.

A 'coaching session' is just a structured way in which you and your sponsor/upline work together to help YOU DISCOVER and LEARN.

Remember we 'coach' you. We are not 'expert' trainers, our job is to help you learn. It is your responsibility to learn, not ours to 'train'.

Each session must start with a TRUST stage to build the relationship, get the learner talking and create a positive state of mind.

To learn the core skills, then you need to help to **DISCOVER your learning needs**: what you don't know and cannot do.

And then you need to **LEARN**. You need the answers to those learning needs explained and or demonstrated. You then need to practice with a coach or someone else in the business [role-play] and then you need feedback.

In fact you will need repetitive practice with feedback in a secure coaching environment to build the confidence necessary to the 'practice' with live prospects.

Each session must finish with a **COMMIT** stage to determine the Learning Goals to achieve through achieving Activity Goals.

This is also the time to discuss the support, such as events and incentives, and to **BOOK** the next Coaching session.

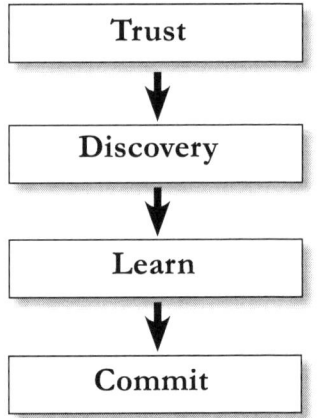

After the coaching session, you will take some action with prospects to learn the skills. Your activity. Obviously, you may also create some results yet it is important to remember the focus of your activity is to learn. You will make mistakes yet this is the only way you learn a skill.

- And then you will do another Coaching Session and PRACTICE.
- Then you take action and PRACTICE with prospects.
- Then another coaching session.
- Then practice with prospects.

SESSION - PRACTICE - SESSION - PRACTICE

The more sessions you have, the you learn and build confidence. The more you practice, the faster you will learn.

COACHING SESSION

PRACTICE

This is how you build skills the fastest!
This is how you build your confidence the fastest!
You never learn in just one session.
You need to have coaching sessions as often as possible.

What types of Coaching session?

There are three types of coaching session:

1.   Face-to-face session.

An individual session and the most effective as you can focus on exactly what needs to be learnt. They should last no more than 60 minutes.

2.   Telephone session.

Also covers internet based communications like Skype. An individual session and 95% of your sessions will be on the telephone. Must not last more than 30 minutes.

3.   Group Coach session.

Also called a home workshop. 3-10 people in someone's home practicing skills together. Lasts no longer than 60 minutes.

Follows same structure as individual sessions.

People love attending because they are short, fun, social and effective. This is NOT a 'sizzle' as it has structure and direction.

They are the most effective training environment in Network Marketing and a new person should be running their own first

Group session within a month of joining!

There is a specific process that everyone can learn to master these three sessions. When you know how to run them, you can help anyone learn and become independent. It guarantees their success!

> If you knew that you can help anyone and everyone succeed, how many people could you sponsor?

> [and the crowd yelled] **Everyone!**

Become a Rising Star

To learn how to run these coaching sessions, you need to subscribe to the Rising Star Programme.

This low-cost online programme will explain exactly how to run these sessions so within 24 hours you will KNOW you can succeed.

www.risingstarsecrets.com

Eliminating Time Wasters

The great benefit of Network Marketing is that it is a very low cost opportunity and everyone can join.

The problem with Network Marketing is that it is a very low cost opportunity and everyone can join!

Time is your biggest asset and people who are not prepared to do the work required to be successful will waste your time.

We NEVER restrict people from joining because we don't know WHO is prepared to do the work. Yes, sponsoring is a 'numbers game'.

The **ONLY** way to determine if **YOU** are worth the investment of coaching time, is will you do a coaching session?

The coaching session requires you to learn skills and take action. It requires you to master your system.

If you are not prepared to do this then your sponsor and upline will stop working with you and you will have to learn on your own.

Chances of success?

We know this is 2%!

In fact, its lower because your success is based on you running coaching sessions with your successline people and why would they do this if you do not?!

Measuring Progress

To build confidence, you must know you are progressing.

To start off, you obviously cannot measure performance. They are NOT competent or confident! So what you do is measure your learning.

Your upline and you will measure your learning in a Coach's Notebook. In this notebook, you measure your knowledge, attitudes and skill levels. Your upline will show you how to do this.

Eventually you can measure your achievement of the competence standard for that skill.

Your goal is to become 100% at this skill THEN you prove to yourself that you are competent. So you will be competent and independent. Your upline's job is nearly complete.

Summary

- Everyone can learn the skills and build confidence

- 98% of people MUST have individual coaching

- Each coaching sessions has the same four step process. Trust - Discovery - Learn - Commit.

- You learn by attending a coaching session - practice - session - practice - session

- If you dont want to attend a coaching session or take the action agreed to learn then expect your upline to STOP working with you.

- Your job is to run a coaching session - face-face, telephone and group coaching sessions

- You learn how to coach on www.risingstarsecrets.com

- We determine who are time-wasters by who will do coaching sessions

- Measure your progress by measuring learning in a Coaching Notebook.

Lesson Twelve
Build your Success Team

Let's remember the basic theory.

You sponsor three Builders and you coach them to sponsor three Builders and you Coach them to Coach their people to sponsor three Builders. Your 3 gets 9 [3 x 3] who get 27 [9 x 3]. [You may build in 2's or 4's, it's the theory that matters here].

Now if everyone is working the system. So the 27 will get 81, who get 243 and so on. Thus you will create the Numbers necessary to have a lot of people from which you earn a little bit of money.

A little bit of money from a lot of people = a lot of money!

The lesson to learn here is that you should focus on the first levels of Builders and become competent in the skills of sponsoring and coaching. In turn they will give you thousands of people simply through the Power of Duplication.

You should focus on those you sponsor and the people they sponsor. These Builders are part of your **Success Team**. If they do their job, you will create Duplication and you will make a fortune.

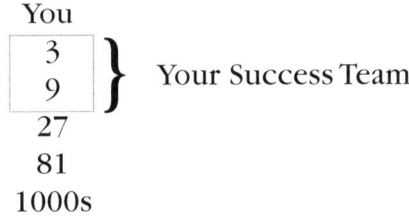

You
3
9
27
81
1000s
} Your Success Team

Third generation pulse

Each level of Builders are called a generation. The first two levels are your Success Team. What happens on your third generation will reveal how well your Success Team is performing. They are like the pulse of your network.

If your 3rd generation is booming with lots of customer volume, new Builders and coaching, then your Success Team are doing their job.

Your future will be fantastic.

Key Points
- Focus on your first two levels of Builders [called Generations] and if they are strong, they will give you a network in thousands. They are called your Success Team

- Performance on your 3rd generation is like a pulse of your Success Team.

Lesson Thirteen
Create a TidalWave to become a Leader

Every leader in every Network company in the world achieved their LEADERSHIP RANK by using what is called the TidalWave strategy. It is the ONLY strategy that works.

A TidalWave is the largest wave on the ocean.

Creating a large network is like building a wave. If the wave is too small, you never reach the Leadership Ranks. Achieving the Leadership Ranks means you must create momentum which creates the TidalWave.

The difference between theory and reality

We all wish that life would be as easy as the theory! If only it was just like making a cake; add the right ingredients, put in the oven for the right amount of time, and hey presto! A perfect cake!

The Theory

In Network Marketing, the theory is that you sponsor a few people, and then the Power of Duplication means that your organisation eventually explodes in Numbers so you achieve a LEADER rank and a big income.

It's so simple that anyone can achieve this and success is just a matter of time. In fact, many think that if you work 5-10 hours per week PART-TIME, a LEADER rank can be achieved.

The Reality!

The reality is that the theory was correct until the part about working a few hours per week Part-time and you can achieve leadership rank.

Unfortunately, people rarely do what is logical. To create any success, especially in a 'people based' business, we always have to overcome some natural negative laws of nature.

Between you and success in Network Marketing are three natural forces: Confusion, Attrition and Gravity. The only way to overcome them is with the use of the TidalWave strategy.

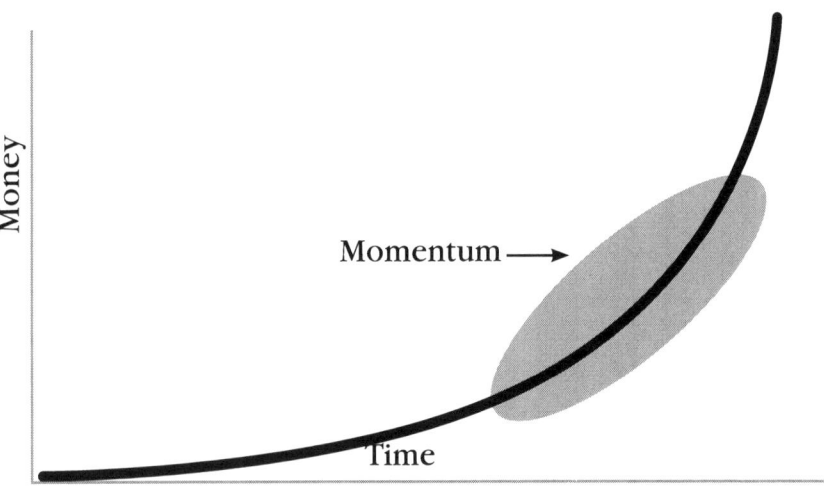

Network Income curve

Income Grows with Numbers

The graph above shows the theory of how a network income should grow.

Initially growth is slow as the Numbers accumulating are small. Your motivation and confidence in your opportunity keeps you working.

Eventually the true Power of Duplication takes charge and the numbers get exciting very quickly. After 128 is 256, 512, 1024!

Momentum

When the Power of Duplication takes control of your Network, it will grow with little or no effort on your part. You have achieved a state of growth called MOMENTUM.

This is a growth stage where one day you have 100 people and two months later there are 200 people. You discover that you have a booming team that you never knew existed. Your confidence and enjoyment in your business explodes. So does your income. There is nothing as exciting as your Network in Momentum!

Momentum is a state of Growth
when your network grows by itself

The important Point is that the ONLY way to achieve a LEADER Rank is to create Momentum growth in your network.

MOMENTUM = LEADERSHIP INCOME

Pushing the Flywheel

The key to momentum is **Sponsoring Speed.**

As the diagram describes the Sponsoring Process, you can see it works like a Flywheel. The faster the Flywheel spins the more people are sponsored.

This does not mean you ignore creating customer volume or learning skills, it just means that driving the Flywheel to sponsor numbers into your team, is the Number 1 priority for success. As I said at the very start, FIRST you must reach a Leadership Rank. Without numbers, you can never earn enough money.

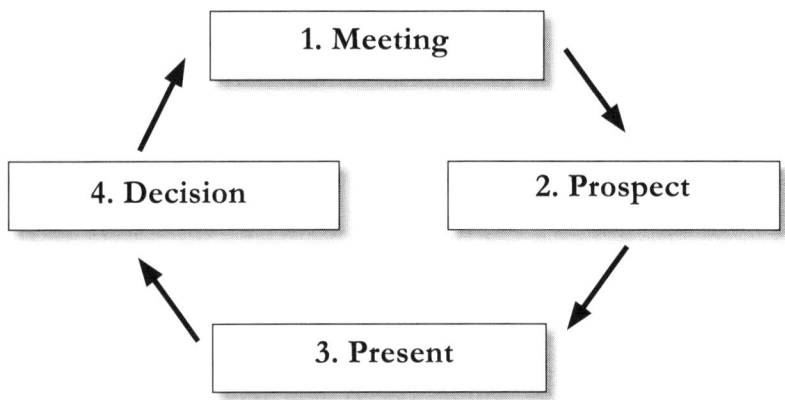

CONFUSION, ATTRITION AND GRAVITY ARE THE THREE ENEMIES OF MOMENTUM.

Unfortunately, natural forces of human nature, Confusion, Attrition and Gravity, will slow sponsoring speed and destroy your chance of Momentum. The TidalWave strategy is how you overcome them.

Confusion

Confusion kills confidence. A confused person takes little or no action!

It is important that when you explain your 'system', ie what someone needs to do to be successful, that you do it in a way that is not too detailed or incomplete.

If its too detailed, people wonder where to start or if they will ever succeed. If you explain your system too simply, they may get started quickly yet in a few weeks they will recognise that they do not have the 'whole story' and get confused.
You overcome confusion through 100% Success Coaching.

The biggest source of momentum-killing confusion is not knowing how to coach properly. If you do not know how to coach a new person, your lack of confidence will rapidly be passed onto your new person and they will stop working.

Attrition

'Attrition' [Churn or dropout] is the natural loss of people within an organisation. Every month, for whatever reason, some people will decide to stop working their business. You cannot stop them and don't waste too much energy trying to do so.

The problem with Attrition is that it reduces the number of people in your team who are involved with Sponsoring. In addition to this, your new people will not sponsor a lot of people as they are still learning.

Excessive Attrition

People will always stop working for their own reasons [natural attrition]. The challenge is 'excessive' attrition which is when people stop because of something you are doing. The failure rate becomes too high it undermines confidence and this makes attrition worse.

The simple solution is coaching! It fixes this problem immediately.

Speed is the key

Natural Attrition only causes a problem in your team if you are growing too slowly. If your network is only sponsoring people at a slow rate then all you will do is replace the people you lost [your natural attrition]. You will never tap into the Power of Duplication.

To achieve Momentum, your business must be growing much faster than the natural Attrition

Gravity

It will not shock you to know that most people are not naturally optimistic. They are sceptical about success. They procrastinate when they should be working.

These are the negative emotional forces that create the excuses and the justification for a lack of action. They raise questions about the potential of this opportunity to dull the excitement.

These negative emotional forces create what we call **Gravity** – a natural force that can stop your network 'flying' with Momentum.

The negative emotions of 'Gravity' can slow your growth so much that the Attrition has the power to stop you creating Momentum.

**Gravity and Attrition work together
to destroy network growth**

Overcoming Gravity

The best way to learn to overcome gravity and thus overcome the power of Attrition, is to think of other man-made things that fly. An aeroplane or a rocket ship. An aeroplane does not naturally fly into the air, the force of gravity keeps it on the ground.

The only way it flies is by using another law of nature to overcome gravity.

By gaining enough speed in the TAKEOFF the aeroplane taps into the force of aero-dynamics and thus is able to fly.

When is the most ENERGY used in an airplane flight? In the TAKEOFF to overcome the force of gravity. It is speed that overcomes Gravity.

YOU HAVE TO TAKEOFF

In Network Marketing, 'speed' is sponsoring speed. It's getting the Flywheel to spin fast enough to Takeoff.

To overcome the negative emotions of 'gravity', you use more powerful natural inspirational forces. The excitement of freedom. Of wealth and the time to enjoy it. Of a 'Desire' for a better life.

If you truly believed in this force, you would be working as hard as possible. You would invest the MAXIMUM ENERGY today. You will take MASSIVE ACTION AND URGENCY!

Urgency and Action communicates Belief

By applying maximum energy, you will communicate an URGENCY of action that will be felt by people. Urgency in business is unusual as it means either crisis or massive opportunity. In this case, you will naturally communicate that you have a fantastic opportunity. You will build people's BELIEF about the power of your opportunity to change their lives. They will start to believe they truly can 'Get Rich'.

DO IT NOW!

Fulltime Attitude

If you believed that your opportunity could help you achieve your dreams, would you be working with a casual, time does not matter, PART-TIME ATTITUDE?

Of course not!

You would be working every hour that God gave.

You would be working with a FULLTIME ATTITUDE.

From the minute you woke till you fell asleep [and probably while dreaming as well], you would be thinking, talking, breathing your business. 24/7.

This does not mean you stop any current work or family commitments. It just means until you get your Network into Momentum, you have a FULLTIME attitude. You apply MAXIMUM EFFORT to create MASSIVE ACTION.

Your urgent action creates urgent action in others in your team so that you get sponsoring speed and thus your network takes off! It goes into momentum. You create the Tidalwave!

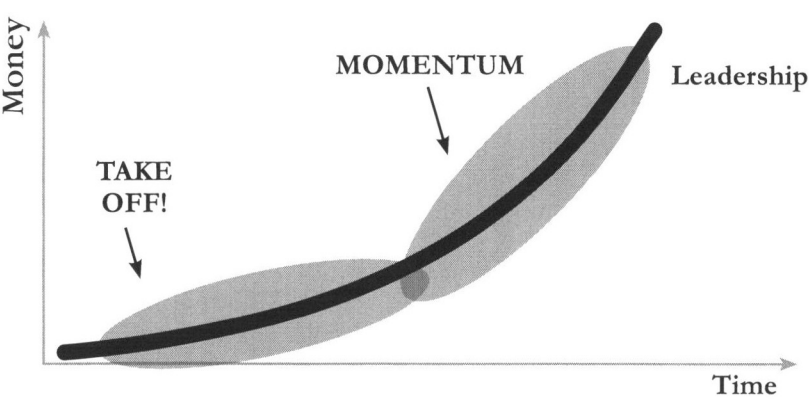

Creating the TidalWave!

Is this normal?

Of course.

Every career, business or opportunity with a massive reward takes an initial period of massive action. It is the natural way of things.

How long?

The massive action is during the period of the TAKEOFF. For some people, it is six months. The average is probably twelve months.

You cannot go on 100% power forever and nor do you have to. Once your network is in Momentum, the Power of Duplication takes over to drive your network until you reach a LEADERSHIP RANK.

Making the FULLTIME Decision!

Having a FULLTIME attitude and working every second you have spare on your business for 12 months is a big commitment. The rewards are worth it, financially, emotionally and spiritually YET are you ready to make this DECISION?

> *"One decision can change your life forever"*
> **Tony Robbins**

I am not ready!

At the start, many people are not ready to make the 'Fulltime Decision'. The reason is nearly always due to your confidence in success with your opportunity.

In this situation, you have two choices: either purely focus on getting customers or enter the **Confidence** programme. The purpose of the programme is to BUILD CONFIDENCE.

In the **Confidence** programme, you are working as much time as you can commit to learning skills. You will be getting customers, sponsoring people and coaching them on the system. You will be attending as many events, workshops and coaching sessions as you can to build your confidence.

You will make some money yet nothing like those who have achieved LEADER positions. This does not matter as you understand why this is and your goal is to create confidence.

Have Fun!

I know that many people just love being involved with Network Marketing on this 'part-time' mentality. They love the products, the people, the positive events and building confidence. It is the most fun business to be involved in!

That's great. You are welcomed and respected.

You can make some money.

The only thing to remember is that you cannot expect to reach the leadership ranks with this approach.

What happens if you have someone who has made the FULLTIME decision?

If you are in the Confidence programme and someone in your team has made the Decision to GO FULLTIME. Fantastic!

The only issue here is that you are unlikely to be a good coach to them as you do not know what it's like to be working with a Fulltime attitude.

In this case, Network Marketing has a great system in the Upline concept. In your Upline, there will be people who have achieved LEADER status so must have created momentum. Call them immediately; explain the situation and they will help you. They are paid by the company on the volume created by your team for this exact situation!

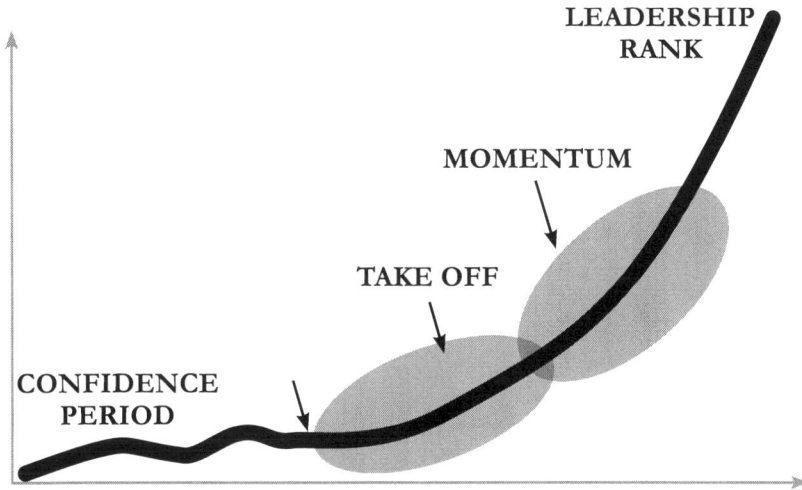

Key Points

- The only way to reach a Leadership Rank is with Momentum.
- Momentum growth is when the Power of Duplication takes control of your network.
- You drive the Flywheel to create Momentum.
- Confusion kills confidence. Coaching overcomes confusion.
- Natural attrition means people will naturally stop working. You must grow faster than your attrition. Coaching wdramatically reduces attrition.
- Gravity is the natural negative attitudes that stop people working.
- Churn and gravity slow the network growth so it never taps into the Power of Duplication and thus kills the change of momentum.
- Only Sponsoring speed through Urgent and Enthusiastic Action will ensure that Sponsoring speed is fast enough. So the Flywheel turns fast enough to create Momentum.
- Only a FULLTIME attitude creates urgency and enthusiasm. Working with a FULLTIME attitude requires a clear DECISION.
- With a FULLTIME attitude you enter the TAKEOFF period.
- If you are not ready to make the Decision, then you are in the Confidence Programme. Learning skills and making a small amount of money.

Lesson Fourteen
Surviving the Dip!

Motivation comes from within

Every journey to success has challenges. Some say that it is the challenges that you overcome that make the 'journey' worthwhile.

To be successful in all things, you must be motivated. As we explained in Lesson Two, the key to motivation in Network Marketing is confidence. Confidence releases the motivation you have within.

Your Story

One of the first actions you should be asked to undertake is the development of what is often called your 'story' or 'lifestyle story' which taps into the HEAVEN/HELL theory of motivation.

It will explain the key positive dream motivators of your future [HEAVEN] and the key negative motivators of your past and present [HELL]. This is a short [say 5minute] explanation of why you have joined your company. It will explain a little bit about your past especially frustrations [your HELL] and what you intend to get out of the business [your HEAVEN]. It is very important to be able to confidently and inspirationally talk to someone about your business and it will motivate you.

ACTION – Write your story NOW

The Motivation Dip

Normally its useful to know the challenges before you start so you know how to deal with them when they arise. Maybe you can take action to avoid the challenge in the first place.

To succeed in Network Marketing you have to get through the Dip

Over 95% of people who quit their Network business do so in the Dip. They quit because they didn't know it was coming or did not know how to get through it. If you follow exactly what we tell you, you will survive the Dip and be ready to create 100% Motivation to make the decision to go into Momentum [see Lesson 12]

The Science of Motivation

Before you learn how to survive the Dip, you need to learn about
1.   Motivation Levels,
2.   Motivation Cycles and
3.   the Dark Zone.

Motivation Level

The best way to think of your motivation is as a level from 0% to 100%. For every aspect of your life, you will have a different motivational level. You can be 0% motivated about one area of your life and 100% about another area. When it comes to your Network business, you should know:

1. Everyone joins a Network business with their <u>motivation at a certain level.</u>
2. Motivation level does not equal action. Your motivation to do something does not equal the action you take. To convert <u>motivation into action, you need confidence.</u>
3. The most powerful influence on your motivation is your <u>motivational cycle.</u>

Motivation Cycle

Driving your Motivation Level, in any subject you are focused on, is your Motivational Cycle. It is either positive or negative. The Motivational Cycle starts moving as soon as you start doing something. It is either a virtuous spiral pushing your motivation up or a vicious spiral where motivation just gets worse and worse.

Positive cycle of motivation

NEW CONFIDENCE

POSITIVE FEEDBACK   **MASSIVE ACTION**

STRONG RESULTS

Negative cycle of motivation

LACK OF CONFIDENCE

UNSATISFYING FEEDBACK

HESITANT ATTEMPTS

POOR RESULTS

Key Points

1. **Motivation Cycles begin at standstill.** When you start your Network business, your Motivation Level will be at a certain percentage [say 60%] yet your Motivation Cycle is not turning.

2. **Action creates a direction.** As soon as you start doing something in your business the cycle will start moving positive or negative. What must be understood is that the direction of your motivation cycle, negative or positive, takes a bit of time to get going. It can start positive and then go negative or the other way. The first few days do not matter so much yet it helps to start off as positively as possible [by taking massive action].

3. **The cycle is a flywheel.** Your motivation cycle is like a flywheel. It takes time to get moving yet eventually develops its own momentum and will spin on its own unless you slow it down.

4. **Hard to change.** Like a flywheel, once your Motivation Cycle has momentum one way, it is hard to turn around. This is why

it's hard to get highly motivated people down or to re-motivate negative people.

5. **It has influence on people.** Your motivation will influence people, especially those with low motivation levels or a slowly turning cycle [either direction].They will accelerate or slow a cycle. If you are new and someone has developed a negative cycle in business get out of the way, they will take you down! Talk to leaders, they know what to do.

Understanding the Dip

The graph below charts the two most likely paths your motivation will follow in your Network Marketing business. Route A is the Dream Route which approximately 2% of people achieve. Route B is the most likely route that will end with you either on the pathway to 100% Success or stopping.

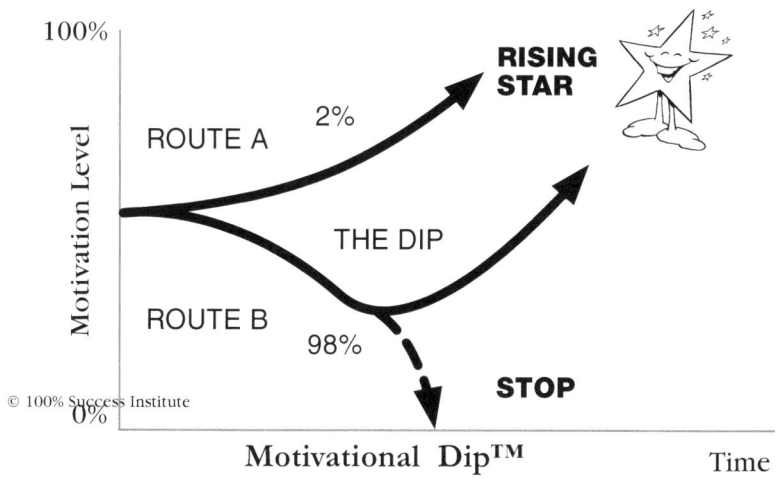

103

Route A

Route A is the DREAM route. You take Massive Action and it quickly produces Strong Results which starts a fast moving positive Motivation Cycle [refer Positive Cycle of Motivation].

Your confidence soars so you take greater action which produces continued positive results. Your Motivation Cycle is spinning in a positive way so keep driving it hard and you will achieve momentum thus become the next leader in your company! Achieving Momentum is covered in Lesson 13 – Tidalwave.

**Take Massive Action for the Greatest
Chance at Success**

Route B

The vast majority of people (98%) will take Route B. They will not have the confidence to take massive action or they will take massive action and it does not produce Strong Results because they are not competent.

They will start learning and will make mistakes. They will get responses from people they did not expect. It may take longer to learn skills than you thought. Whatever happens, your motivation drops and you enter The Motivational Dip!

Reality Check – Before anyone panics, we should remember that when you have learnt anything in your life, you get a motivational dip when you start. No skill is as easy to learn as you imagined.

TWO OUTCOMES

When you enter the Dip there are only one of two outcomes; you survive the Dip or you stop. What determines the outcome is what happens to your Motivational Cycle.

Outcome 1 - Stopping

You enter the Dip and motivation drops. If you allow your Motivation Cycle to turn negative, your motivation will continue to drop. Confidence drops so actions become more hesitant leading to poorer results so eventually your motivation is so low, you stop working. Which in Network Marketing terms, means you quit. You may keep buying products, maybe even supply products to customers, yet you have stopped building a network so have quit.

The chances of you reactivating in the business after stopping are nearly zero as your attitude to the business will be negative.

If you do develop a negative cycle, the answer is the same as Surviving the Dip.

Outcome 2 - Surviving the Dip

People who follow the 100% Success strategy and have a professional coach/upline will survive the Dip.

Everyone else will quit.

Surviving the Dip is simple.

You have to get your Motivational Cycle turning positively by building your confidence by learning skills. It takes time yet eventually, it will lift your motivation up.

The key to this is FOCUS.

The Right Focus

One of the most important keys to success in Network Marketing is stated on page 59, under the title 'What about my Goals?' There it states that there are actually three types of goals: Results, Learning and Activity.

If you join the business and focus on Results Goals it is highly likely that you will be disappointed because you will be trying to achieve results when you are still incompetent.

Sounds a stupid thing to do?

You would be amazed how many people do!

They focus on Results Goals, don't achieve them fast enough and thus it undermines their confidence and their motivational cycle turns negative. They continue to focus on Results Goals with dropping confidence which reduces their motivation, commitment and action taken. So they stop working. They quit.

Focus on Learning and Activity Goals = Success

If you are focused on learning then you are focused on Learning and Activity Goals, rather than Results Goals. You can be achieving 100% of Learning and Activity Goals, be making excellent progress, feel fantastic about your business yet not be earning much if anything at all!

Smart networkers, and those with smart coaches, can measure their improvement in knowledge, ability in skills and delivery of activity. It proves they are succeeding by building capability to perform.

Increasing Success Ratio

The achievement of Learning and Activity Goals means that the new Networker develops a Positive Motivation Cycle. As your competence and confidence increases so will the ratio of successful presentations as a percentage of your total; your Success Ratio. More people will become customers, more presentations will turn into new Networkers.

Eventually, you will be able to focus solely on Results Goals and will focus on passing your Competence Standards, which you will pass. You will become a competent, confident and thus INDEPENDENT networker!

Through the Wall

You will often hear Network Leaders saying 'Success in this business is not a sprint, it is more like a marathon.'

Anyone who has successfully run a marathon will talk about the joy of completion, they rarely tell you about 'The Wall'. The Wall is when people quit and the Dip is the Network Marketing equivalent. To feel the joy of successfully running a marathon, you must run through 'the wall'. Once you've done it, it's actually no big deal. You quickly forget what it was like.

Some mothers say it is like child-birth, a nightmare at the time yet quickly forgotten in the joy of motherhood.

DREAM AND DARK ZONES

There is one last important concept concerning motivation, you need to know about called the Dream and Dark Zones.

As you can see described on the graph below there is a level of Motivation where you move from the Dark Zone to the Dream Zone. This level is different for everyone.

Some people go into the Dip AND they enter their Dark Zone so you need to know what to do.

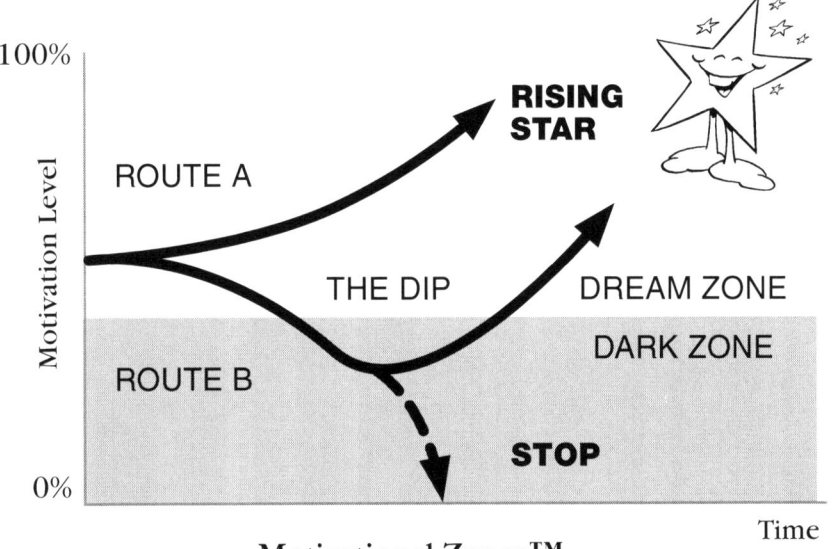

Motivational Zones™

The Dream Zone is when you can be motivated by 'Dream Building'. These are inspirational motivational influences that help you 'dream' of a better future. It pulls you along and helps lift your motivation.

The Dark Zone is when Dream Building has no effective impact. Your state of mind and motivational level means that you are unable to believe in your 'dreams' enough for them to motivate you into sufficient action.

You may get excited for an hour or a day yet take no action. You may come charging out of your company's event inspired for massive action yet the following day, you will be unmotivated.

Getting out of the Dark Zone

The only way to get out of the Dark Zone is working on your Confidence.

- Refer Lesson Two. Review WHY you have made a Smart Decision.
- Review WHAT you must do to be successful. Do you believe you can do this?
- Lastly, Go into massive action learning. Competence will grow quickly driving confidence which puts you back into the Dream Zone again.

Everyone is different
The Dark Zone is a different level for everyone. Some [lucky] people can have low motivation yet still be in the Dream Zone. Some people can be highly motivated yet not be in the Dream Zone. This is very much determined by your personality type and life experiences.

100% ACTION
The obvious advice for all new people is to take MASSIVE ACTION on Activity and Learning Goals. Focus on measuring your Learning rather than your Performance.

Key Points

- To succeed in Network Marketing you have to get through the Dip.

- Your motivation is in a level from 0% to 100%

- To convert motivation into action, you need confidence

- Your level of motivation to Network Marketing is specific and is eventually driven by your Motivation Cycle.

- A few new people take massive action and achieve great results which drives their success

- Most people begin learning and experience a drop in motivation into the Dip.

- Those that focus on Results normally create a Negative Motivation Cycle and so will Stop.

- Those that focus on Confidence through Learning can produce a Positive Motivation Cycle whilst in the Dip and so climb out of the Dip and succeed in the long term.

- There is a level of Motivation for all people below which inspirational 'dream-building' is not effective; they sink from the Dream Zone to the Dark Zone. In the Dark Zone, motivation is based on Confidence building mainly through Learning.

Special Mention. Whilst we have taught this phenomenon for years calling it many names normally 'The Hump', the 'Dip' is a much better name and was shamelessly adapted from a fantastic book called The Dip by Seth Godin. Buy his book as it is fantastic.

*The Motivation Dip is a trademark of 100% Success Institute Ltd

You may wonder, *'Do I have everything to be successful?'* ie. all the knowledge and support. If this question is not answered you may feel insecure and blame your mistakes on a lack of information and support. You will then search endlessly online and/or listen to so-called 'gurus' that will just make you more confused and insecure!

Relax, the answer is simple. Here is the complete 'Learning' BASICS, called 'The Knowledge', you need to become 'independent', are as follows:

1. Company and product information. Come from your company. They are the experts.

2. Networking Industry information. Comes from reading/ listening to 100% Confidence book/CD. That's all you need! You can easily go online and read endless 'reports' about the state of the 'Networking / MLM' industry yet the author/promoters NEVER know the full story and are just trying to confuse you to lure you to their opportunities in an underhand manner.

3. Basic Network Building theory. It's in this book!

4. Basic Training / Learning Knowledge on your business administration, Sponsoring and Retailing is supplied by your upline organization/company. It will be in some form of manual/s, video, audio and online combination. ONLY ask your upline!

5. Coaching knowledge. This is a specialist area and it's important to be 'up-to-date'. All the basic knowledge and latest developments are in Rising Star Programme. It is inexpensive and access is online 24/7. All personal coaching is provided by your upline.

6. Motivation, attitude and inspiration. Your organization will recommend and/or deliver a programme of motivational/ inspirational resources. Start with one simple book, CD or download today. No high cost personal development programmes are need to be successful if you use the 100% Success strategy with upline support.

7. Specialist knowledge, such as personal branding, marketing, etc. If provided by someone outside your organization, only take on recommendation of your upline.

More detail on these areas is on **www.100percentknowledge. com**

100% Success Summary

This book started with the comment... *What would you do if you knew you couldn't fail?*

This question should now inspire you as we hope that you now understand the 100% Success strategy and recognize it is the key to your guaranteed success.

We trust that there is no confusion. Discuss any confused areas with your sponsor. Remember confusion is the death of all success in Network Marketing.

Let's summarise the whole concept...

You join a Network Marketing company and decide you want to be a Networker. Success is based on a combination of Customer Volume, Numbers and Competence.

The reason everyone can succeed as a Networker is five simple reasons:

1. Everyone has a **system based on three skills that they can learn**
2. They **learn until they are competent** which they will know by passing a knowledge test and achieving set performance standards
3. The **tests and standards are achievable by everyone** as the business is not based on 'super-sales people' or 'super-recruiters'. The sales strategy is Inspirational Sales. The key to success is in everyone doing a small amount regularly.

4. Competence means that everyone has the confidence to keep working which means that the network will tap into the power of Duplication
5. Eventually you will build the confidence to make the decision to go 'fulltime' and drive your network into Momentum to achieve Leadership Rank

> The Purpose of the 100% Success approach
> is to give a 100% chance of success
> through becoming a competent networker
> to make you ready to become a team leader.

Build confidence

With understanding, your confidence should be stronger. Confidence is the key to success in Network Marketing.
- It releases motivation
- It produces action
- It is the key to communication, especially with people you know.

Confidence is based on:
 a. Smart decision on products
 b. Smart decision on business
 c. Understanding the system will work for you
 d. Competence in skills

Do you understand what 'rich' means?

Money and time freedom to develop those relationships and experiences that make life fulfilled. It's not millions. It is achievable by anyone in Network Marketing when you have built a **Leadership Income.**

You build a Leadership Income in two steps, firstly you achieve a Leadership Rank by getting your network into momentum using the TidalWave strategy. Then by ensuring there is sufficient customer volume and competence.

And if you want to make the millions and own the Ferraris, then this is also possible. If you can reach a Leadership Income, then with the same skills and a lot more effort, SuperStar status is achievable.

LEARN SKILLS FIRST

The initial focus of everyone is to LEARN the system. This is how the 100% Success strategy works and then three key skills: Retail, Sponsor and Coach.

Everyone can learn the three skills with enough practice thus everyone can succeed in this business.

GO FULLTIME

Creating the TidalWave for momentum is a simple matter of a FullTime attitude. You create excitement and urgency through massive 24/7 action. This overcomes the natural churn and gravity that slows the Flywheel from turning fast enough to create momentum.

CONFIDENCE PROGRAMME

The challenge for many people will be having the confidence to adopt a FullTime attitude to create momentum.

If you are not ready then all you need to do is to focus on learning skills. You will make some money, you will build your confidence and this business has many other non-financial benefits to enjoy. You are part of the Confidence Programme.

READY TO GO FULLTIME?

If you are ready to make the Decision to go fulltime then fantastic! A world of possibilities are ahead of you and if you follow the 100% success strategy and your sponsors advice you will become a leader.

Our last piece of advice is to enjoy the process.

This is an amazing industry due to its positive attitude on life and its belief in the potential of anyone to succeed.

We believe that anyone has the natural power inside to achieve success and our system does not judge you or discriminate against you. So you, even you, have a 100% chance of success.

What next?
- Immediately attend a 100% Success Workshop or similar workshop run by your upline where they will show you what to say to your warm market and how to coach someone after they join. This is vital as it will give you the confidence to

KNOW that you can be successful in the business. You need this to release sufficient motivation to go into massive action!

- Register on the Rising Star Coaching website www. risingstarsecrets.com. Here you will learn the basic knowledge about how to coach someone in just a few hours. You will gain the confidence to know that you can help everyone succeed which is so important when you talk to your warm market.
- Now read the 100% Success Coach book again so you know what to do when you sponsor someone to guarantee their success
- It's time to commit massive action to learn the core knowledge and skills. This means an enormous amount of practice with your sponsor and/or in workshops.
- When you are confident, call a number of your close friends and family and go around to practice on them. Take your sponsor with you. Don't worry if they buy/join or not, the point is just to practice.

The last point is to believe in your success. Everything is possible in this business and dreams often come true!

Good luck

Ed

The Parable of the Golden Goose

New people in all things are impatient. The time it takes to learn all things always seems too long. Take a lesson from the parable of the Golden Goose.

A farmer discovered that one of his geese laid solid gold eggs. He was overjoyed and every day cashed in the golden egg.

The problem was that the goose took a day to lay each egg. One each day and some days, it did not lay any.

Eventually his greed and impatience got the better of him and he killed the goose to get at the half created egg it was growing inside its body. Obviously, the goose never laid another golden egg.

Developing a network is like raising Golden Geese. You must be patient. Not only do they produce golden eggs yet some hatch into more Golden Egg laying Geese. It takes time for them to produce. They must learn skills, they must build confidence.

Try to short-cut the process and you will kill the geese off. Develop it properly and you will have a growing flock and a growing hoard of golden eggs.

Putting 100% Success to Work

The 100% Success Strategy is the foundation underneath your system. The WHAT to do, rather than the HOW to do [the three skills].

To help you understand how to perform the skills in your system, I have outlined some useful points.

PROSPECTING

Whether you are a Retailer or Networker, you need to 'Prospect' for people to do a presentation on either Product or Business. It is a vital skill to master.

Warm Market First

The Networking business is based on using our contacts to build our business. We approach our 'warm market'. This means we must believe in the value of our products and business. When we talk to people we know, they will know if we believe through our natural communication. Our enthusiasm and confidence. You don't have to say very much at all.

Cold Market always

Go where you normally go, do what you normally do and take your business with you!

You will never run out of prospects if you take your product and business opportunity with you in your daily life. Maybe carry a product. Certainly always bring literature with you.

Do I need scripts?

Sales scripts detail exactly what to say to different sorts of people. Under-confident people especially like the idea of scripts not realizing that with a script you will worry if you are getting the words right. This means your communication will be flat and uninspiring! You kill the most important aspect of a discussion – your confidence and enthusiasm. All you need are a <u>few key points</u> to explain, which incidentally some leaders call a 'script'.

Stories Sell, Facts tell

Facts are interesting yet they do not inspire people. Stories or testimonials of how a product or the business impacts you, is always more effective. If you do not have any personal stories, use those of other people. Your sponsor and system will provide these for you.

Using Tools

Sponsor or Retail Tools, such as brochures, CDs or DVDs, will never be as powerful as your personal enthusiasm YET they are proven to be worth the investment. They give you an edge as they provide clear professional information.

Most successful top people use them heavily. That's the key; make sure you use a lot of them. No rationing! This is advertising. Wherever possible, use tools developed for your local markets rather than other countries.

COMMUNICATION

Change State

People will naturally have a positive or negative 'state of mind' when you meet them. If it is negative then it is impossible for them to be excited about your opportunity - product or business. You cannot feel HOPE with a negative state of mind.

Change their state using very positive language, especially in your greeting. When they ask you 'How are you?' Instead of 'I'm OK', say 'I'm Fantastic!' or 'Sensational' or 'Awesome'. Use a smile and shake their hand if possible. The state change will be immediate!

RETAIL

Two types of customer

Nearly all products sold in Network Marketing are repeatable so once they have used the product once; we want them to keep buying month after month. The only reason someone will keep buying is because they think OR know the product has value to them. There is a HUGE difference between 'think' and 'know' and thus there are two types of customer; a *Tryer* and a *Buyer*.

- A *Tryer* is a customer who is just 'trying' your product. You have explained and inspired them to 'try' the product. They 'think' the product may have value yet are not convinced. You have to 'promote' the product to them every time. If you do not promote the product, they will stop using it.

- A 'Buyer' is a customer who has decided that they want to keep using your product. With no promotion on your part or the company, they will seek to buy the product. A Buyer may keep using your product for years and thus have enormous value to you. A Buyer will also consider buying more products, recommend your products or consider becoming a Networker.

The goal of Retail is to build and maintain a large group of Customer Buyers.

> Key Point – your job with a customer is not complete until they become a Buyer or decide never to buy again. This is why FOLLOW UP is so important.

SPONSOR

'Referral' income disaster

If you use a product and refer it to a friend, are you paid by the company for the new customer? No.

So the idea of saying 'Hey join this business and make money from referrals' sounds great yet it actually compromises the whole concept of a referral. Being paid for referrals is called 'selling'.

FREQUENTLY ASKED QUESTIONS

Is this selling?

If the prospect ask this question, they are worried about putting pressure on their friends and family or they do not believe/or want to 'sell'.

This is a good question because you need to know that there are two types of selling.

One is called Professional Selling which uses pressure to get a customer. We deal with people we already have a relationship with, so would never use pressure.

We use Inspirational Sales where we use the quality of the product and customer stories to inspire them to try the product.'

Is this pyramid selling?

When someone asks about 'pyramid selling' or 'is this legal?' Do not ask them what they mean as they will not know and you will only make them feel stupid. They will only ask this question because they have experienced or heard about the high failure rate in Network Marketing in the Establishment sector of its Lifecycle. If someone asks the 'Is this Pyramid Selling?' question, simply reply...

'Of course not, yet I assume by asking this question, you may have heard about the failure rate in Network Marketing in the old days? [Everyone nods or agrees]

It was true, like all new industries in their pioneering stage; we had a high failure rate. I am excited because we have evolved our system to be based on skills so now everyone can succeed.'

Read the book or listen to the audio - **100% Confidence Why Network Marketing is booming again** for the clear explanation on what has happened in the past of Network Marketing, to give you 100% confidence in the future of this industry.

COACH

Coaching is the highest paid and worst performed skill by Builders. It is the highest paid because this is the skill that develops the Network. All 'sponsoring' does is build a base of people to grow from. It is the worst performed skill because most people are confused about what they need to do.

Discipline

Coaching is simple to learn yet you must have the discipline to follow the coaching process and not get caught up in the emotions and distractions of your new people.

Start to Finish

Coaching is the job of the Sponsor. It starts the minute your new person joins your team and finishes the day they have proven they are competent.

Coaching sessions

All communication with your team must be considered as a Coaching Session. In the session, your sole objective is to help them learn the skills.

Learning how to coach

You need to register on Rising Star Coaching. It's low cost and in a few hours you will know the basics. www.risingstarsecrets.com

Role-play and workshops

The greatest tool to coaching is role-play and workshops. Role-play is you and your new person practicing the skills. This practice will rapidly build the confidence and competence of new people. They are a secure environment for learning. Workshops are just a group of people doing role-play and getting feedback.

Take notes

It is vital that you take notes on the development of each key person in your team. It allows you to become more effective with your time. Use Coaching sheets to measure your people's improvement.

SELF-DEVELOPMENT

'Self' or 'personal' development is the development of your character. Self development covers everything from your values through to your attitudes and goal-setting. Every successful network marketing leader will confirm that self-development is a critical area for success.

Our Advice is:

• Start using self development products today. Read and listen to self development products everyday. Get rid of the music in your car and MP3 players and play self-development material. Attend self development events when you can.

- Focus on products that directly relate to your business today. Basic goal-setting, attitudes and communication are simple subjects to start with.

- Start with a simple CD or book. CD/MP3 is best.

- Lastly, use products that relate the best to you. Women should use products from women authors if possible. Forget the 'deep reflection' products and focus on 'woman creating success' type products. In a similar style, wherever possible buy products from local authors so the message communicates more effectively to you.

And most of all ENJOY the process. Self-development should be a wonderful journey of discovery and improvement.

MEETINGS AND EVENTS

Meetings and Events are not training sessions. You can't coach skills in meetings. Skills are learnt in interactive workshops.

Meetings and Events are VITAL for inspiration and confidence. Everyone MUST attend EVERY Meeting and Event. They are that important. It is NOT negotiable.

RECOGNITION

Nothing builds confidence and releases motivation more than appreciation, praise and recognition. You cannot do enough of it. Do it often.

WHY WOMEN LOVE 100% SUCCESS

Like it or not, God designed men for performance and women for relationships.

In the Recruiting Game strategy, success is based on performance: recruiting and motivating others to recruit. You join and are sent out to perform. 'Training' is based on providing information, ideas and inspiration on how to perform. There is no class interaction, no ability to discuss concerns. There are few developed relationships.

Women LOVE the 100% Success strategy because it is based on relationships and interactive learning. Performance is secondary until competence is developed. Success is based on learning skills without pressure and helping others learn skills. 'Training' is through interactive coaching, role-play and workshops. The interaction means people can discuss concerns.

Why do men LOVE 100% Success strategy? Because it delivers solutions to higher performance. It is more logical.

At his presidential inauguration speech Nelson Mandela said...

"Our deepest fear is not that we are inadequate.

Our deepest fear is that we are powerful beyond measure.

It is not our darkness, but our light that frightens us.

We ask ourselves 'Who am I to be so brilliant, gorgeous, talented and fabulous?'

Actually, who are we not to be?

Your playing small doesn't serve the world. There's nothing enlightened about shrinking so that other people won't feel insecure around you.

We are born to make manifest the glory of God that is within us;

It is in everyone!

And as we let our light shine, we unconsciously give other people permission to do the same.

As we are liberated from our own fear our presence automatically liberates others!"

ABOUT Ed Ludbrook
The Network Coach

Ed has a unique role in the global Network Marketing industry as a Network Coach and has coached over 100 organisations and 100,000's of people across the world since 1994. He is Europe's leading author and speaker on Network Marketing who has sold over 2 million books in 20 languages.

For 15 years, Ed has been pioneering competence-based [100% Success] training systems with Network Marketing. He is passionate about the delivering significantly higher success rates because it will transform this industry and empower everyone involved to achieve their dreams. He presents the 100% Success TV show [www.100percentsuccess.tv] to entertain and educate people in dynamic 5 minute shows.

Ed's true passion is Leadership training and he has trained Network Leaders across the world for many years. Due to the normal leadership approaches not being effective in this unique Network environment, he developed the 100% Leadership approach. His leadership blog is www.100percentleadership.com

Raised in New Zealand, Edward graduated from Royal Military College Duntroon, Australia's prestigious army officer university. He served in the NZ Army Engineers then moved to London where he worked in investment banking and strategic consultancy before focusing on the Network Marketing industry.

When the industry has embraced his 100% Success vision based on the core concepts of competence based learning and leadership he intends to retire, help save the planet from global warming and produce a fantastic Rose wine to celebrate life with his family in the sun.

To hire Ed as the keynote speaker at your next conference, email his office on admin@ludbrook.com

The 100% Success
TV show

Tidalwave!

How to create momentum to get rich fast with the Eight Secrets form the Asian Masters.

Creating momentum in Network Marketing is the only way you will become a TEAM Leader. There is no luck involved if you follow the TidalWave formula that Ed has developed coaching numerous organisations around the world.

100% Success Coach

Learning the skill that creates 100% Success

The only way to create competence is through effective coaching. Not performance coaching, competence coaching. They are different and the skill process is specific to Network Marketing.

Based on 12 years of trial and error within organisations around the world, this book is the bible on coaching and thus success in Network Marketing. IT explains WHAT and HOW to coach in all situations with all sorts of Networkers and Retailers. This includes, telephone, international and difficult person coaching. It includes how to run home workshops. It works will all programmes and systems.